To my fellow
May the force
be with you!

Regards,
Helen

GOD MEETS ZEUS

HELEN GOCHIS

This novel is a work of fiction. Names, events, characters, corporations, institutions, organizations, and locations in this work are the products of the author's imagination or, if real, are used fictionally.

Acknowledgement

Thank you God for my lengthy and fruitful existence on Earth and for every member of my extended family, past and present.

Dedicated to those who are attempting

to balance the Nature of the Universe

with the needs of everyone on Earth

GOD

MEETS

ZEUS

ZEUS

MEETING OF THE MINDS

The scene is the home of Zeus on Mt. Olympus, the ancient hilltop complex of palaces located on the highest mountain peak in Greece well above the white clouds. This heavenly home of the pantheon of gods still exists as does Zeus, the Supreme Leader of the Gods.

The bronze foundation of the stone temple is decorated with gold and marble and glitters in the sunlight. In the nearby stables, the immortal horses whinny as they tire of waiting for the call to fly, which has not come for more than eight hundred years.

The golden gates are well guarded by three of the twelve goddesses of the hours of the day.

It hardly seems necessary since, other than in the eyes of the gods, Mt. Olympus was said to have been only a vision in the minds of man.

GOD MEETS ZEUS

It is now the year 2018.

Seated on his throne in the central hall, Zeus is handed a gold cup filled to the brim with Ambrosia, the magical nectar of the gods.

The drink is credited with maintaining Zeus' vitality and immortality. It has been brought to him by an automaton, a metal figure made by Hephaestus, one of the gods. His automatons were known to have the capacity to think as well as the mobility of man.

Placing his once meaningful scepter aside casually, Zeus drinks slowly and sighs.

There's a breeze coming through the open spaces between the ornate Doric columns that surround the hall. Shivering slightly, Zeus pulls his white wrap up over his uncovered shoulders .He turns his head toward a bright light flashing and the wind seems to whisper in his ear.

"MY, YOU LOOK BORED. I SEE YOU ARE STILL IMMORTAL. DOES AMBROSIA NO LONGER LIFT YOUR SPIRITS AS IT ONCE DID?"

Zeus clenches his empty right fist and instinctively considers throwing one of his famous thunderbolts in the direction of the light, but fears his once powerful weapon no longer has much strength.

He watches as the bright light dims and a sense of calm rises in the air.

"DO NOT BE AFRAID. I HAVE COME TO TALK."

"I fear no one, but is this truly the voice of God, the God who dethroned me and scorned me for nearly a thousand years? Have you come now to gloat?"

Zeus is apprehensive but there is much he has bottled up for years and he cannot control his tongue.

"You are silent but do not deny that you were the instrument of my demise. My bitterness rises and sarcasm seizes my tongue but I must ask you for what reason do you enter my thoughts?

The sky is bright blue and the sun is shining. You reign supreme. What problems could you possibly have?"

The light brightens and the voice grows a bit louder. Branches of a nearby fig tree shake and leaves float to the ground as the air in the room whirls and God's voice echoes against the golden walls.

"I FEAR THAT THE PERFECT WORLD THAT I CREATED WILL CEASE TO EXIST IF THE MORTALS CONTINUE ALONG THE PATH THEY HAVE TAKEN."

PANTHEON OF GREEK GODS

A Greek poet named Homer wrote a history of the gods that were worshiped in ancient Greece. Until then the tales of love and war, of power and defeat, and the escapades of the gods on Mt. Olympus had been repeated only by mouth, one person to another, one generation to the next.

His stories were of the gods and the turbulent time they lived in long before the birth of Christ. His "Iliad" and Odyssey" are still widely read today.

"Our world began," he once wrote, "with Gaea the earth, followed by the virgin birth of her son, Uranus the heavens, and their children the Titans."

The legend continues with Uranus being overthrown by his son, Cronus, the god of time.

In a violent clash of power, Cronus' three sons overtook him and then drew lots to divide the universe.

GOD MEETS ZEUS

Poseidon drew the Sea, Hades the World beneath the Earth, and Zeus the Heavens. Zeus then led all the many gods, who were called Olympians. He is an immortal god.

Perhaps it is the millions of words that have been written and studied about this place and its gods that have kept him and Mount Olympus afloat.

Zeus is silent for a moment after hearing the plea in God's voice.

"I well understand your concern about the world you created. Although my time to rule has passed, there is no limit to the earthly events that disturb my peaceful sleep.

"Surely you do not look to me to assist you in straightening out your world after forcing me from my celestial kingdom to make room for your Son, Jesus.

"I admit it was a smart move on your part, but I deserve all the credit for the idea of having children by mortal women.

"In my case it was lust, my frailty at matters of the heart and the body. In your case it was carefully calculated to reduce my powers."

Zeus goes on complaining about his lost kingdom, now raising his voice.

"I frowned when I heard of the chosen one to bear the child. She was a young innocent and it took me a while to figure out your plan. It became clear as statues of me were defaced and temples left in ruins."

“ENOUGH!”

There is fierceness in the voice and the light is blinding. This time the fig tree is bent over and touches the ground. The calmness is completely extinguished.

“YOU WERE BUT ONE IN A LONG LINE OF MINOR DEITIES. SINCE THE BEGINNING THERE WERE GODS OF THE STORM AND THE WIND, OF THE SKY, THE WATERS, OF LOVE AND WAR. EVEN THE SUN THAT SHINED DOWN WAS BOWED TO.

“STILL YOUNG, YOU STEPPED INTO BIG SHOES. SURELY YOU KNEW OF BA’AL WHO WIELDED HIS THUNDERBOLT BEFORE YOU.

“HE WAS ACCEPTED BY THE ANCIENT HEBREWS FOR MANY YEARS AND THE SEA-GOING PHOENICIANS SPREAD HIS NAME WIDELY.

“THE LIST OF THOSE CALLED GOD IS LONG AND I ALLOWED EACH OF THEM TO SHARE IN THE GLORY.

“YET IT DID NOT STOP THE SLOW PROGRESSION LEADING TO THE POOR STATE OF THE WORLD TODAY.”

“This is not news to me. I have often thought to intercede, but my powers are limited to sending suggestions through the waves of thought, most often in dreams that are ignored in the light of day.”

Zeus unwisely continues the debate.

"But again why did you get rid of me? I was doing so well. We could have negotiated a deal.

"My gods inspired the people in their knowledge of science, agriculture, philosophy and so much more. "Yes, we fought a few wars but we nurtured human life.

"During the original Olympics, which by the way have now become something more involved in politics than a sport of men honoring gods, all arms were laid down and the people came together in peace for the games.

"Greece was evolving and would have remained one of the greatest civilizations, not simply a major tourist destination."

"DID YOU NOT SEE THAT YOUR GODS SUFFERED FROM THE SAME FAULTS AS TODAY'S LEADERS OF THE WORLD? I SPEAK OF THINGS SUCH AS ENVY, GREED, CRUELTY AND SELFISHNESS?

"YOU DID NOT TRY TO CONTROL THE CONSEQUENCES OF THESE FAULTS. IN FACT YOU DID MUCH TO ENCOURAGE EVENTS IN YOUR TIME BY SETTING POOR EXAMPLES YOURSELF."

Zeus is subdued, but still cannot hold his tongue.

"I am not used to being spoken to as an unruly child.

"There was no conflict as to who was the supreme god in my time and there were many accomplishments.

"The gods set good examples, especially my daughter, Athena. I still delight at the sight of the olive groves and remember when she first introduced them to the Greeks."

"We developed democracy, a theory of government never before successful in the ancient world."

The light continues to flicker, expanding and contracting as though God is taking deep breaths.

Fearing he has overstepped, Zeus is finally silent.

"I AM NOT HERE TO CONGRATULATE YOU ON SUCH ACHIEVEMENTS SINCE THEY WERE THE DEEDS I EXPECTED.

"NOR DO I WISH TO CHIDE YOU FOR PAST TRANSGRESSIONS OR ANYTHING THAT THE GODS MAY HAVE DONE WITH OR WITHOUT YOUR BLESSING.

"AS YOU VENTED THE BITTERNESS AND SARCASM YOU HAVE AMASSED, I WAS VERY PATIENT. HOWEVER I MUST NOW ADJUST SOME RECOLLECTIONS IN YOUR MIND.

"I REMIND YOU THAT WHEN ONE OF YOUR LEADERS SOUGHT REVENGE AND CAME TO HIS BROTHER FOR HELP, THE CALL FOR ACTION WAS ANSWERED FROM ALL PARTS OF YOUR KINGDOM.

THE PRICE TAG

"WARRIORS GATHERED READY WITH SWORDS AND SHIELDS. THE YOUTH OF TWO NATIONS FOUGHT OUT OF LOYALTY AND HONOR FOR TEN YEARS.

"You are speaking of the conflict in Troy. In fact, I was very pleased with the response. I felt great pride when the ships came from so many parts of the empire. They all set sail to revenge the abduction of my brother Menaleos' wife, Helen, by Paris of Troy.

"There is no regret when you fight for the right cause. Hundreds of ships did come at once and carried thousands of warriors.

"Although many consider it a mythical story it has never been forgotten and has been immortalized many times over.

"DID YOU NOT FORESEE THAT YOUR ACTIONS WOULD BRING ON YOUR OWN DOWNFALL? WERE YOU NOT AWARE THAT WHEN MENELAUS WENT FOR ASSISTANCE TO AGAMEMNON HIS POWERFUL WARLORD BROTHER THAT THEY MAY HAVE SEEN IT AS A CHANCE TO PILLAGE, TAKE CAPTIVES AS SLAVES, AND STEAL THE WEALTH OF TROY?"

"You are mistaken. Surely, Menelaus sought nothing but revenge."

"SO YOU THOUGHT NAIVELY THAT THE WAR WAS CAUSED SIMPLY BY THE VANITY OF YOUR GODDESSES.

"YOU PREDICTED VICTORY FOR THE GREEKS, ALTHOUGH YOU KNEW THEN THAT IT WOULD BE A LONG PROTRACTED WAR AND MANY THOUSANDS WOULD DIE.

"THE PEOPLE WERE LEFT TO FEND FOR THEMSELVES FOR MANY YEARS. IT IS NOT SURPRISING THAT THERE WAS WIDESPREAD FAMINE FOLLOWED BY MASS MIGRATION.

"NOT LONG AFTER THAT WAS WHEN CHRISTIANITY AND ISLAM SWEPT AWAY WHAT WAS LEFT OF YOUR KINGDOM. YOU PLAYED A BIG PART BY SIMPLY NOT DOING ANYTHING TO STOP THE WAR."

Zeus steps down from his throne and paces back and forth before he replies.

His cheeks are flushed by shame as he acknowledges the possibility of his error of judgment, but he still continues to defend his actions.

"These were honorable warriors who swore allegiance to their King. They were obliged to live and die by that pledge. They did what was right.

"That is what happens in war."

"RIGHTEOUSNESS IS VERY OFTEN THE EXCUSE GIVEN FOR THE GREED AND PRIDE OF THE LEADERS AND ONE THAT MOST OFTEN LEADS TO WAR. UNFORTUNATELY, NEW LEADERS DID NOT BRING NEW MORALS. THE WARS OF TODAY FOLLOW MUCH THE SAME PATTERN."

"And who are you to criticize? How many hundreds of thousands of warriors have come to your gates?"

The bright light dims and God's reply is softly whispered.

"YES, WE BOTH REMEMBER THESE THINGS AND CAN ARGUE FAULT FOR AGES.

"HOWEVER MY WISH IS TO ADDRESS THE STATE OF THE WORLD TODAY AND HOW WE MIGHT ALTER THE PATH TO WARS MOST OFTEN FOLLOWED BY MAN."

Subdued by God's gentle words, and no longer doubting his sincerity, Zeus lowers his head and responds.

"I admit you have humbled me. Perhaps there is some truth to all you say. How can I be of service now?"

"YOUR VERY TRANSGRESSIONS HAVE SUGGESTED THERE MAY BE SOME HOPE FOR THE WORLD. YOU HAVE GIVEN YOUR LIFE FORCE TO ENABLE MORTAL WOMEN TO BEAR CHILDREN WHO, BY YOUR ACTIONS, WERE SOMETIMES DEEMED DEMIGODS.

"***True, there were many who carried my seed."***

"THEY WERE NOT IMMORTAL, AND ALTHOUGH IT MAY BE DIMINISHED, PERHAPS THE VERY POWER OF YOUR SEED HAS BEEN CARRIED DOWN OVER THE GENERATIONS AND STILL EXISTS.

"These thoughts have never occurred to me. What wonderful images you have placed in my mind. Perhaps a young Apollo, or even a replica of my wife, Hera."

"LET US FOLLOW THE LIVES OF A NUMBER OF THEM. THOSE WE CHOOSE WILL REPRESENT THE POPULATION OF THE WORLD.

"IF THEY SWAY FROM THE SINLESS PATH SET FOR THEM AT BIRTH, AS MANY MORTALS HAVE DONE BEFORE THEM, I WILL HAVE THE ANSWER I SEEK.

"THE PAST CANNOT BE REWRITTEN, BUT WE CAN TRY TO INFLUENCE CHANGE.

"WE WILL SEEK EVIDENCE TO PROVE THERE IS HOPE FOR THE FUTURE OF THE WORLD."

"Influencing and meddling in the affairs of mortals are not new to me. Your thoughts are negative but indeed your proposition does interest me.

"I will not claim to believe that any young person, demi-god or not, would be able to succeed in convincing you that this world is worth saving, but I will follow your lead."

"WE WILL USE EXAMPLES FROM THE PAST AND THOUGHTS TO GUIDE THEM BACK, BUT THE CHOICES THEY MAKE WILL BE THEIRS, AS WILL THE CONSEQUENCES THEY SUFFER.

"JESUS HAD TWELVE DISCIPLES WITH A MISSION TO CHANGE THE WORLD.

"PERHAPS TWELVE YOUNG MORTALS WILL BE ABLE TO FILTER THE ACTIONS OF THE WORLD AND ASSIST IN MY DECISION."

"Indeed my pantheon consisted of twelve gods also. A dozen mortals would seem an appropriate choice."

"DONE. WE SHALL CHOOSE TWELVE MORTALS WHO MAY SERVE TO INFUENCE MY DECISION REGARDING EARTH.

"HOWEVER, I WILL WITHHOLD MY JUDGMENT REGARDING THE FUTURE OF THE EARTH FOR ONLY A SHORT TIME."

ATHENA

THE CHOSEN ONES

Searching for a mortal who is beautiful, pure in heart and body and also a demi-god descendant, Zeus is instinctively drawn by his native tongue to an area called Astoria.

Situated across the East River from fast paced Manhattan in the borough of Queens, Astoria is often called the heart of the Greek-American settlement in New York City.

"What pleasant sounds. Why this shopkeeper has the very olives I have eaten since my daughter Athena first introduced the olive tree.

"He is speaking Greek to the young boy as he hands him a sweet, and the boy has responded in Greek. I am pleased that the Greek language has survived so well, even though this dialect is a bit strange."

Zeus continues searching the busy streets as daylight is replaced by the dark of night and he sees the light of flickering candles.

"There seems to be a procession coming from that building with all those people carrying candles behind a flower bedecked bier. Perhaps it is the funeral of a very important man."

"SO YOU RECOGNIZE THE LANGUAGE AND THE CEREMONY AND THEN CHOOSE TO IGNORE THE VERY LARGE CROSS.

"IT SEEMS YOUR MIND DOES NOT ACKNOWLEDGE THAT THOSE GREEKS ARE CELEBRATING THE RESURRECTION OF CHRIST."

"I do see that now, however the pangs of jealousy strike and overcome me as I remember the huge crowds that once worshipped me."

The lovely oval face of a young girl glowing in the light of the candle she's carrying from church grabs Zeus' attention. He was admiring her beauty when he heard her mother beckoning her.

"Athena, stay close. It's very crowded."

Tears fill Zeus' eyes as recognition of his favorite daughter's name and memories of her overtake him and blot out thoughts of the rest of the crowd.

He feels an overwhelming desire to keep track of the seventeen year old mortal.

Athena Pappas has a twin brother, George. Her grandparents came to America as immigrants from Greece after the first world war. Steve Pappas, Athena's father, mentions often that he wanted to name the twins Artemis and Apollo, as in Greek mythology.

However his wife, Maria, argued and would only agree to her favorite girl's name, Athena.

This pleases Zeus, both for her father's thought and her mother's action.

George is destined from birth to take over the family diner. Athena is admired for her beauty and good nature, but as a girl, is left to make her own decisions within the narrow choices her family approves.

"I can hardly believe my good fortune finding this mortal."

Zeus is pleased by what he's learned of the young demi-goddess, which is how he now considers Athena.

She attends a school named Townsend Harris High School in nearby Flushing. He sees her as an athlete, at least it looked that way to him as he watched her doing acrobatics wearing a red and gold uniform at the school football stadium.

"They are calling this team the Harrisites, which sounds ancient, but they do not play football as I know it and keep knocking each other over and hugging the ball. It's a wonder they can move with all that clothing on."

There was talk among the girls of final tests and graduating, but most conversations he chose to listen to mentioned expensive dresses and a planned event.

"That gathering would be a good chance to see my Athena in her royal beauty."

It's easy for Zeus to continue thinking of the girl as his own daughter.

"ZEUS, YOU SEEM TO BE COMPLETELY PREOCCUPIED. ARE WE NOT GOING FORWARD?

"REMEMBER WE MUST FIND TWELVE MORTAL DEMI-GODS WHO CAN CONVINCE ME THAT THE WORLD WILL CHANGE FOR THE BETTER."

Zeus was determined to include Athena as one of the chosen but is not quite ready to inform God of his choice. He selfishly wants to share in her actions without interference if he should desire to help her.

"I have made my choice and will finalize it at a gathering of young people that takes place on Friday night."

"HAVE YOU INDEED SUCCEEDED IN TRACING SOMEONE WHO CARRIES THE BLOOD OF A DEMI-GOD?"

The cunning Zeus tries to disguise his growing feeling that indeed Athena is a demi-goddess and somehow a direct descendant of his own child.

"The thread of life has been woven loosely over the centuries. I believe we can be confident that at least a drop of ancient Greek blood is evident in the mortals of the present generation, regardless of their lineage.

Zeus realizes how obvious is his intent to favor Athena and quickly amends his statement.

"But I will also insist that regardless of their culture all mortals are potential candidates. After all they will represent humanity and their actions will determine if mortals deserve to continue to exist."

"YOU SKIRT MY QUESTION ABOUT FINDING A DEMI-GOD BUT VERY WELL. YOU MAY PICK FIRST.

"I WILL NOT INTERFERE WITH THE FIRST ONE YOU CHOOSE. I WILL WAIT MY TURN. IN FACT I WILL REMAIN UNAWARE OF

THE MORTAL'S EXISTENCE SO YOU HAVE A FREE HAND. I WILL SEE THE RESULTS EVENTUALLY."

"I bow to your negotiating prowess. Obviously you wish to have the same right of secrecy in your first choice. I'll grant your wish this time. However we will limit this cloud covering to only the first two mortals."

With an agreed upon veil that will cover his own actions, God decides on a method of choosing his first candidate, taking care to avoid breaking his agreement. His thoughts are clear.

"THERE MAY WELL BE TIMES WHERE MY JUDGMENT AND PLAN OF ACTION WILL DIFFER FROM THAT OF ZEUS. I MUST SAFEGUARD THE OUTCOME WITHOUT BREAKING MY PROMISE.

"I WILL KEEP MY BARGAIN, NEITHER GUIDING NOR ADVISING, BUT MY FIRST CHOICE WILL REPRESENT ME IN THE FORM OF THE HOLY SPIRIT THEREFORE I NEED NOT WORRY ABOUT THE PURITY OF HIS ACTIONS."

THE GATHERING

“THIS IS A CONFUSING SIGHT. THERE ARE MORE BALLOONS FLOATING IN THIS GYMNASIUM THAN CLOUDS IN THE SKY. THE COLORS OF THE BALLOONS ARE REFLECTED IN THE DRESS OF THE FEMALES AND THE MALES EITHER MATCH THEM OR ARE DRESSED FOR A FUNERAL. THE MUSIC IS SO LOUD THAT WORDS MUST BE WHISPERED IN EARS TO BE HEARD.”

“I like the balloons, and the ones announcing the year are clever. I remember children blowing up the bladders of sheep but only to fill with water.”

“THAT GROUP OF MALES HUDDLED IN THE CORNER LOOK TO BE FIT.

"THEY ARE CONSTANTLY SHOVING EACH OTHER, BUT THEIR LAUGHTER AND CAMERADERIE ARE A JOY TO WATCH.

"THAT ONE IN CONVERSATION WITH A PROFESSOR MAY BE OF MORE INTEREST."

Zeus has spotted Athena.

"While you listen to him, I'll just look around for other possible choices."

"Yes, Mr. Johnson, I am still very interested in pursuing a career in astronomy. I was only eight when my grandfather first took me to the planetarium. He was born in Greece and told me how the stars were named in Greek mythology. When he pointed out each one and named them, I felt like I was in church looking up at heaven."

"I THINK HE'LL BE QUITE SUITABLE AS MY FIRST CHOICE. HE HAS NOBLE THOUGHTS TO STUDY THE HEAVENS AND HIS BEING OF GREEK DESCENT SHOULD MAKE HIM ACCEPTABLE TO ZEUS."

"But I was really hooked when we went to the American Museum of Natural History and saw a movie about a voyage from Earth into the Universe. I was still young and glanced over at my grandfather when the narrator's voice sounded like that of Sheriff Woody of the Toy Story movie.

We both laughed when he explained that it was the actor Tom Hanks whose voice was used for both."

The professor also laughed, although God did not quite understand what was funny.

"My grandfather shared my interest in the stars until he passed away two years ago and made me promise to continue reaching for them.

"I've been checking out colleges and I've made application to Texas A&M."

"That's a very good school, Michael."

"Yes. They have the best observatory center. It has full gigabit internet connectivity and powerful computers that can conduct complex processing of recorded images and radio sounds.

"They're able to detect new stars and planetary bodies."

Now God does laugh.

"LOTS OF BIG WORDS, BUT SPOTTING STARS IS AN ANCIENT ART AND NO BIG DEAL."

"I think you're wise in choosing a school and concentrating on a subject you're really interested in.

"Come to my classroom on Monday and I'll write a recommendation. Your excellent grades should help. Let me know how you make out."

Although Zeus body is not physically present in the gymnasium of the school, his ears are closely tuned to the words spoken to Athena by her friend.

"Athena, your dress is fantastic. You look like a Greek goddess wrapped in white tissue paper."

"Please, Judith, don't say that too loud.

My mother insisted on sewing my dress. I have to admit it's pretty but the Greek thing is over the top."

Zeus is puzzled by Athena's comments but his mind is cluttered with flashing images He pictures the young girl in the armor his Athena wore, the thunderbolt in her hand when he indulged her wishes, the owl on her shoulder and a pale light shining on her beauty.

He trusts that God will stick to their bargain and tries to clear his mind of what is transpiring, but he finds it difficult to completely shut out the sight of young Athena.

"AS PROMISED, ONCE MICHAEL HAS MY INSTRUCTIONS IN HIS MIND, I WILL GIVE UP CONTROL AND HE WILL BE ON HIS OWN, BUT STILL A HOLY SPIRIT. NO NEED TO MENTION IT TO ZEUS."

God has already decided on Michael, but at the moment he is afraid that he may have to break his word in order to pinpoint Zeus first choice and direct Michael appropriately. However the light shining on the young girl is making it obvious.

"I have made my first choice."

"I TOO HAVE MADE MINE."

COLORS OF THE RAINBOW

"I've noticed the slanted eyes of many students and how dark their hair is, while their skin tone shows favoritism with the sun god."

Remembering a young man chatting with his first choice, and not wanting to show special interest in his connection with Michael, God casually points out Bill Parker.

"SHOULD WE NOT INCLUDE ONE? THE BOY THERE HAS DARK HAIR, A ROUND FACE AND HIS EYES SLANT, ALTHOUGH THEY ARE A LIGHT COLOR NOT USUALLY ASSOCIATED WITH HIS SKIN TONE.

"Yes, let's include him. Now that you mention skin, there are many mortals in the world with different color skin, eyes of various shades and even some with differently textured hair, and that doesn't cover the pink and purple hues evident here tonight.

"How did this come about? Was it in your master plan? You know this has become a very big part of your problem with Earth. It seems it has come to be an excuse to discriminate and subdue other mortals."

"MY INTENTION WAS TO INHABIT THE UNIVERSE FLOATING HIGH AMONGST THE STARS WITH MANKIND. THEY WERE GIVEN THE EARTH AND INTELLECT. MEN AND WOMEN WERE LEFT ON THEIR OWN TO SPREAD OUT OVER THIS VAST GLOBE "

"Isn't it ironic then that caravans led by camels through ancient trade routes that were established to spread the work of the lowly worm have led to the homogenization of mankind and so many problems?"

Zeus hears a sigh and knows that he is irritating God with his constant questioning.

"It seems the thought of a lowly worm upsetting the plan touches a nerve.

"LET'S MOVE ON. SURELY THERE ARE OTHER MORTALS IN THIS GROUP WHO QUALIFY FOR OUR NEEDS.

"That tall fellow reminds me of Memnon who fought so bravely at Troy. Surely his ancestors have come from the same distant land of the black Moors. They are calling him Maurice. Will we agree to him?"

"YES, A WARRIOR OF THE PRESENT TIME IS APPROPRIATE."

"That tall girl standing near him looks as if she might be his sister, although her skin tone is lighter."

"SHE IS NOT HIS SISTER, BUT SHE IS TALL AS HER CHEROKEE NAME IMPLIES. I DOUBT HER ANCESTRY CHART WOULD SHOW THE BLOOD OF ONE OF YOUR GODS, BUT IT RUNS DEEP INTO THE ROOTS OF THIS CONTINENT.

"HER MOTHER IS OF THE CHEROKEE TRIBE OF NATIVE AMERICANS AND FATHER IS A MOHAWK OF THE FIRST NATION IN CANADA.

"This knowledge of the girl surprises me. Why such interest? Had you already picked her out?"

"NO, BUT I WOULD GLADLY DO SO, DEMI-GOD OR NOT. HER FATHER IS WELL KNOWN TO ME FOR HIS HEROIC DEEDS. HE WAS AN IRON WORKER, ONE OF MANY OF MOHAWK ANCESTRY USUALLY GIVEN TASKS FOR THEIR TOLERANCE OF HEIGHT.

"WORKING ATOP A NEARBY BUILDING, HE WATCHED ONE OF THE PLANES MAKE ITS FATAL DESCENT DESTROYING THE WORLD TRADE CENTER IN NEW YORK CITY.

"HE AND HIS FELLOW WORKERS RAN TO FIND SURVIVORS. THEY HELPED MANY TO ESCAPE THE DISASTROUS SCENE BUT THEY WERE NOT ALWAYS SUCCESSFUL.

"I HAVE BEEN LISTENING TO MANY PRAYERS FROM BLYTHE'S MOTHER.

"HEROES OFTEN CONFRONT GREAT ANGUISH NOT BEING ABLE TO SAVE EVERYONE AND MANY TIMES CANNOT HANDLE THE RESULTING TRAUMA.

"If Blythe can fill her father's shoes, she will be a good candidate. I would accept her and I also see a young girl that I would like to have participate. The one called Judith over there."

Zeus feels that his Athena should have her friend accompany her on this journey. He still maintains the image of Athena as a goddess, and his goddesses always had helpers.

"HER VERY NAME GRATES AND SENDS CHILLS. IT SOUNDS MUCH LIKE THE FEMININE OF JUDAS. BUT MY SON HAS FORGIVEN ALL SO I WILL NOT OBJECT"

Zeus might not be so pleased with his choice if he knew that Judith tells all that will listen that Jesus saved her life. God on the other hand might find her more to his liking not withstanding her name.

"I would also choose someone who might aspire to the Olympics and that one seems a good choice. Look at his stature and the width of his shoulders. Although his clothing covers the muscular frame, I know he is worthy of becoming a champion."

"YOU MEAN THE ONE DANCING WITH THE MOST BEAUTIFUL GIRL IN THE ROOM?

"Why yes. Her beauty does even surpass that of Aphrodite."

Zeus was actually comparing her to Athena, but decides not to bring attention to his growing interest in her.

"I AGREE WITH THE CHOICE OF THE ATHLETE AND I IMAGINE YOU WILL GO FOR THE FAIREST ONE WITH HIM. SHE SEEMS TO HAVE QUITE A LOT TO SAY."

"Just keep dancing, Henry. I'm sure they're going to break soon to announce the King and Queen.
It's considered very romantic for an engaged couple to be chosen. I'll post the best pictures of us on Instagram.

"Make sure my hair looks good when they place the crown on my head and remember to look surprised when they call our names."

"I *would* be surprised. There are lots of popular kids. Why are you so sure they're going to pick us?"

"Henry, for the umpteenth time, you're the captain of the football team and the best player. They call you 'Hercules' because you're so strong. The cheerleaders can't keep their eyes off you, even though they know you're mine.

"You'll be picked for King for sure, and as for me, I'm the best looking and most popular girl in the Senior Class by far."

Zeus grows impatient with her self-important chatter and does not approve of her treatment of "Hercules."

"She needs to be reminded that there are other beautiful women in the room. My Athena is certainly among them."

Ellen suddenly feels uneasy as she remembers seeing the two cheerleaders that rival her in beauty and might stand in her path to the throne arrive with their handsome escorts. She was confident that she would be chosen Queen, but she now pictures both girls wearing shiny crowns.

She manages to shrug off the image of the other two women. "Anyway, we can't miss. Now wipe the sweat off your forehead."

"I can't help it. This necktie is choking me and the suit is just too hot."

A drum roll starts softly and as it gets louder draws everyone's attention to the stage where the bandleader is heading for the microphone. Two boys are rolling out a long strip of red paper and the dancers move aside to form an aisle down the middle of the dance floor.

Ellen tosses her head to have her long blonde hair fall into the right place on her bare shoulders just as she practiced every night this week. She pats her face, giving her cheeks a glow and wets her lips.

Henry is watching the crowd, looking for his friends. He's hoping to leave soon and change into the comfortable jeans and tee shirt he's stashed in his locker.

Zeus keeps watching as Ellen flings her hair once more in preparation for her big moment.

"That would-be queen certainly has the beauty to turn heads her way and has no modesty.

"Perhaps Aphrodite's name does appear on her ancestry chart.

"THAT MAY BE TRUE, BUT ACTUALLY THE YOUNG MAN IS MY INTEREST AND IS QUITE AN ADONIS HIMSELF."

"I'm surprised you even noticed beauty in the mortal man, but I would match him more to Hercules for his strength."

"I HAVE PROVIDED MUCH BEAUTY IN NATURE AND MAN WAS NO EXCEPTION. THE PERFECTION OF THE HUMAN FORM SHOULD BE ADMIRED AND PROTECTED, NOT DEBASED.

"MANY MORTALS DO NOT RESPECT THE PERFECT FORM I HAVE PROVIDED."

As the drum roll reaches the fever pitch needed to get everyone's close attention, Ellen once more instructs Henry.

"Make sure you look at me and kiss me when they call our names."

As if on her personal cue, their names are announced.

"Congratulations Ellen Jensen and Henry Logan. You are our new King and Queen."

Flustered, Henry pulls at his necktie and squirms to detach his wet shirt from his back.

Ellen squeezes his arm to finally get the kiss she ordered. They walk the red paper carpet to the stage while strips of paper saved by a dance committee member for months are let loose from the ceiling and dime store crowns are placed on the new King and Queen.

Amid cheers from their kingdom they descend the stage and begin the dance they are obliged to do with Ellen smiling smugly,

"I told you we'd win.

"Now smile back at me and go play with your buddies while I give the rest of the boys a chance to dance with the queen."

"Good. I really need to sketch out our plays for the game with the Long Beach Lions next week. We're going to practice all day Sunday but I'll pick you up Sunday night for the movies."

"Okay. Kiss me before you go. Lots of kids are taking pictures."

"HENRY DOES HAVE PROMISE. HE TAKES HIS LEADERSHIP ROLE AS CAPTAIN OF THE FOOTBALL TEAM SERIOUSLY."

"Not as seriously as the beauty takes her role as queen. She may well be a demi-goddess and if she has

inherited any of my daughter Aphrodite's traits we will see mischief and flirtation from this vain beauty. Strength and Vanity, one we hope to nurture and one that may need to be overcome."

"NOW WE MUST CHOOSE AGAIN. LOVE IS VERY IMPORTANT. IT MUST BE NATURALLY FELT BY MOTHERS AND DISPLAYED BY FATHERS SO THAT THE CHILDREN WILL BE SECURE IN THEIR LOVE AND DO THEIR PART TO MAKE THE WORLD BETTER.

"THERE IS A COUPLE THAT ARE DANCING VERY CLOSELY AND VOWING LOVE TO EACH OTHER-PENNY AND DON. LET US INCLUDE THEM.

Zeus is barely listening as his attention has been drawn to the stage.

"Sure, sure, love is very important, but listen to that music. Pan could not have played the flute better than that young girl on stage. Her flute is like magic- it speaks to me of love."

The leader of the small band calls for a short intermission. "Before we let them go let's give them all a big hand."

As they step down from the stage, he calls each name and waves an arm to encourage applause. The flute player, Tayanna, receives very little praise from her audience. The flute is not among their favorite musical instruments. Her high cheek bones are accentuated as she smiles, obviously pleased with her performance.

A friend greets her in Spanish as she reaches the dance floor. "Eso fue genial, that was great."

"Gracias, Max. It is kind of you to take an interest when most of the students think the flute is obsolete and a waste of my time."

"My interest is in you, Tayanna. The flute is just a bonus and you do play very well."

"TAYANNA IS A WISE CHOICE. OUR UNIVERSE HAS ALWAYS TURNED TO MELODIC SOUNDS FOR COMFORT, FOR JOY, AND EVEN FOR THE CALL TO WAR. IT IS A PART OF LIFE.

"IF WE ADD TAYANNA AND MAX, THAT'S TWELVE.

"THAT NUMBER SEEMS FITTING.

"My pantheon dozen enjoyed the admiration of the people and did good works, your twelve disciples took their turn raising the moral standards.

"Now we have the 'chosen dozen' who are being challenged to save the world. The twelve will represent all of mankind."

"INDEED. WE HAVE BY CHANCE FOUND A NATIVE OF THE AMERICAS, A BLACK DESCENDED FROM AFRICA, AN ORIENTAL FROM ASIA AND I'M SURE EACH OF THE OTHERS HAVE ROOTS AROUND THE WORLD."

"But this 'New World' we have chosen from is only five hundred years old, like a teenager compared to other civilizations. Except for natives that inhabited the North American Continent, everyone came after them from somewhere around the world.

"YES AND THE SCRABBLE OF PEOPLE THAT CAME CLUNG HARD AND THRIVED IN THIS NEW PLACE LIKE A SMALL WEED IN A DARK FOREST.

"WE DIGRESS. WE WILL START WHERE WE ARE TODAY NOT IN THE PAST.

"THE TWELVE WILL CARRY THE RESPONSIBILITY TO ALTER THE LIFESPAN OF THE EARTH. WE WILL TAKE THE MEASURE OF EACH ONE."

"The dozen are chosen."

"THE JOURNEY BEGINS."

HADES

"So, Brother, did you plan to completely ignore me while you went about trying to help *him* save his masterpiece?

Zeus recognizes the voice of his brother Hades but tries to ignore him.

"He doesn't call me Brother as you do, and certainly doesn't claim me as kin, but the all-knowing one has his eyes on me I'm sure.

"You haven't looked for me in the shadows lately, but you could not have missed my handiwork displayed in bright color on the news each night.

Zeus is unable to keep ignoring his brother's remarks.

"Your handiwork? Surely you don't take credit for all that. Although many mortals continue to follow you, I know that you have been shoved into the background just as I have."

"My ego was not nearly the size of yours. I chose to cooperate fully.

"When we drew lots I was naïve. I thought the three positions would be equal. Somehow my choice was far below the ladder than yours.

"Far below you-Ha! I am clever with masochistic humor. Let me see. What can I do to amuse myself today?

"No goddesses or court jesters in my realm.

"I guess I must seek comic relief elsewhere and I believe there are plenty of mortals who would volunteer to cheer me.

"You two have lined up those mortals you are confident will come through for you.

"As usual you've been influenced in your choices by beauty and strength, perhaps we can see just how morally strong and inwardly beautiful they really are.

"The actions of mortals sometimes show a cruelty that goes well beyond even my standard.

"The efforts they put forth to torture children repulse me, sometimes even to those of their own flesh. That phrase that is used so often… "Suffer the little chldren…"

"I don't think that's what He had in mind."

"Since when do you defend Him?"

"You will not goad me into any debate. I am merely stating the obvious."

"Well it is very obvious that your spirit is broken, however the challenge is on. I will do all in my power to make sure the mortals screw up.

"Let's see if you and your teammate can turn things around. As far as I can see you don't stand a chance.

"Maybe I'll tempt one of your demi-gods or better goddesses. Perhaps the one you claim as directly descended from Athena.

"In truth, I much prefer the modern Persephone – indeed she is beautiful and tempting.

"No, I won't reveal any plan to you. Just be on your guard. I operate on the fear of what might happen with a strong mixture of jealousy and temptation.

"The prize, after all, is the Universe as we know it. Perhaps it's time for a change."

ON THE FRINGE

"I wish they'd stop looking at me. Those two girls think they're so hot. Bad enough they tease me in class.

"Last week in gym when I tripped over one of their feet, the couch made believe he didn't notice the quick movement that made me fall and everyone just burst out laughing."

Blythe is uncomfortable at the prom. She is six feet tall and full figured, not the average looking student. She has few friends in school and the only person she has spoken to tonight is Jo-Jo and he's not popular either. No one teases him though because they know he carries a knife and is rumored to be a gang member.

"This night and everyone here stinks, Jo-Jo. You're always bragging about having a good time at some party and inviting me to go along. Well, tonight I'm accepting. Let's get out of here."

"You better go home, Blythe. The places I go to are not for you and I don't think you would like the people I run around with."

Blythe had chosen a dark blue dress. Her mother had assured her that the color was slimming. The straight skirt came down to her ankles with the sequined bodice low enough to highlight her ample bosom.

The dress was tight and it was a little difficult to walk, even with the slit on the side. She chose three inch silver high heels that made her even taller.

She wanted to look special tonight, hoping that Maurice would notice her. She's had a crush on him for the past two years, but was too shy to speak to him.

Although she was standing near him now, he didn't look over in her direction. She decided to give up.

"No, I'm not going home, Jo-Jo. All I'll get there is a polite question from my Mom asking if I had a good time, and I'll smile and politely ignore the question like I've done so many times. I can't lie to her and I don't want to disappoint my Dad. He waits up for me too.

"My dad might cry, then hug me and say everything's all right, or he may start yelling and smash things.

"I'm tired of my Dad's mood swings. It's been almost eighteen years and my Mom keeps reminding me what a hero he was on that terrible day – Nine-Eleven, when I wasn't even born.

"I just wish I knew what to expect. It might be a trip to McDonalds or it could be a dark house with him locked in the bathroom and my mother pleading with him at the door."

"If I go home, it'll be worse than this prom charade. I really want to have a good time tonight.

"Let's go. I'm a big girl. I can take care of myself."

Finally agreeing to take her with him, Jo-Jo makes a phone call as they walk to his car.

"Okay, there's a party going on at Big Mike's house. He said I could bring a friend. He's parked on Astoria Boulevard and he asked us to meet there. He's picky about who goes to his parties, but I'm sure he'll welcome us. Want to go?"

"You bet I do." Blythe felt adventurous. She smiled to herself. "My luck is going to change tonight."

Jo-Jo was having second thoughts as they approached the meeting place.

"Big Mike is very generous and treats his women right, but maybe this is not such a good idea. Sometimes these parties get out of hand."

Blythe was barely paying attention to Jo-Jo. She was impressed with the shiny black Lincoln Big Mike was sitting in when she saw him.

He was leaning out the window of the car talking to a woman who walked away when he spotted Blythe and waved his arm to welcome her. He smiled, admiring what he saw.

"So you're a friend of Jo-Jo from school. Why don't you ride with me?"

Blythe was even more impressed when he peeled off a hundred dollar bill from a big roll.

"Go get some cigarettes, Jo-Jo, and meet us at the house later, much later."

"Yeah, okay, but you know she's not like your other girls."

"That's even better. She'll do fine."

Big Mike drove a few minutes to an area that Blythe wasn't familiar with and parked in the driveway of a modest two story frame house.

The lights were on and music was blaring. Blythe was excited and felt very mature.

"C'mon doll. I want you to meet some friends."

Blythe's fancy gown was met with stares from the three scantily dressed girls she was quickly introduced to. The six men stared too. They smiled broadly as their eyes moved up and down her body, stopping at her breasts.

Big Mike was greeted by everyone with the girl named Ginger trying to cling to his empty arm. He shrugged her off and led Blythe away.

"How about a rum and coke, doll?"

Blythe smiled and nodded her head. She didn't want to say she had never had rum before.

Ginger was making her way over to where she was standing.

"Where do you work, honey?" asked Ginger. I don't recognize you. Are you one of Mike's regular girls?

Blythe smiled, unaware of what the question meant. She liked being accepted as one of the girls for a change. She carefully avoided saying that she was a high school senior and only seventeen years old.

Ginger admired her dress and told Blythe she was cool wearing high heels to look even taller.

Big Mike handed her the drink and she took a swallow of it. It may have looked like coke, but the rum was a new taste sensation. She thought it was pretty good.

She hadn't noticed the pills that Big Mike had included in the mix.

"I better sit down." Drinking rum was suddenly not as much fun as she thought it would be. She barely made it to the couch before passing out.

Big Mike took Ginger's arm and led her to the door. "I think it's time for you girls to go to work now, and don't come back in until dawn."

Ginger didn't look happy but did start for the door followed by Didi and Maxine.

"She's kinda sweet, Mike. She's pretty big too. Think you can handle her?"

The men smiled as the girls left and Big Mike winked as he turned to pick up Blythe's limp body and headed for the bedroom.

"Me first, boys."

Although Jo-Jo had hoped for a better ending, he knew the worst was happening when he saw Ginger and the other prostitutes leaving. He parked nearby and waited. Three hours later, two men helped Blythe out the door. She slumped to the sidewalk as they went inside and closed the door.

Jo-Jo pulled up beside Blythe and helped her into his car. She was not unconscious, but had a blank look in her eyes as she crept into the back seat and curled up.

"Where do you live? I'll take you home."

The cry that came out of Blythe's mouth was primeval. She was seeing the scene from afar and it was some other person being violated over and over. Her eyes were not blank, but filled with the horror of the night.

"I can't go home. I can never go home.

"Leave me at the corner there. I see Ginger and that other girl from the house. Maybe they'll let me stay with them."

"You do know what they do for a living? You do know they're prostitutes?"

"That's all I'm good for now."

The other girl walked away and Ginger sat down on the corner with Blythe.

"Why don't you go home? You're just a kid even though you're supersized."

Blythe is quiet and still sitting huddled up.

"You're not in shape to be out here tonight. You do have a home, don't you?"

Blythe finally answers.

"My father's a big hero. My mother lives in fear he'll hurt himself or hurt me when he throws things. If I go home he might do something really crazy like going after Big Mike.

"Mom keeps reminding me what a hero he was on Nine-Eleven. She doesn't stop talking about it but it isn't real to me. As a toddler, I was outside in a playpen most of the time, while my Dad slept a lot. On rainy days, a neighbor took me in. I thought they forgot I was there.

"I never knew what to expect then, but I know they would not want me now. No, I can't go home."

"What about relatives or friends?"

"My relatives are either in Canada or in Oklahoma.

I don't have any friends and being a Native American doesn't open many doors. We got lost when God gave out favors."

Ginger feels sorry for Blythe but doesn't want to show any weakness.

"Anyway, if a man sees you like that he sure won't stop here.

"Tell you what, I have a room that no one else knows about. I hide sometimes and get dead drunk to wipe out a bad time the night before.

"You can crash for a few days, but after that you'll have to earn your keep. I'm sure Big Mike will take you on to work if you cooperate."

"I'd rather die than go near him again."

"Yeah, I hear you kid, but wait until this winter when you're sleeping in a cardboard box on the street and it gets cold. The handouts are few and far between.

"I know a couple of gay guys I can hook you up with but you may have to sell for them. The big money is in heroin.

"The trick is not to get hooked. Although right now I think you would welcome it.

"Here's the key to my room. It's just around the corner over the Indian place. Get some rest."

LOVE CONQUERS ALL

Penny and Don have been going steady since their junior year in high school. It's true that Don has been whispering "I love you" to Penny on the dance floor. She told her best friend that they had gotten more serious since their trip to the beach during spring break. She said she was sure he really loved her.

Don has borrowed his father's station wagon. He plans to leave the prom a bit early, stopping on Lover's Lane and still being able to get Penny home for her one o'clock curfew. Her preacher father has strict rules but they've managed to evade them a few times.

"THE YOUNG MAN IS PLANNING A TRYST AND THE YOUNG LADY WILLINGLY BREAKS HER FATHER'S RULES."

"By the looks of the many automobiles that we see leaving the gathering early, there are many couples with the same idea."

Their favorite parking spot is taken when they arrive at the usual place. Vehicles are close together but prom night always draws more lovers' cars per square foot than can be squeezed onto the short lane.

The lane overlooks nothing. There is no view although describing it on his first invitation Don had mentioned the nice green grass in the nearby park. Astoria is a place of cement sidewalks and buildings built close to them. Anything green grown in the dirt constitutes a view.

Don is sweating. His Dad had told him to save the gas and not use the air conditioning.

He turns off the engine and headlights and hopes no one clips the car's rear end that is sticking out in the road.

There are no other spaces and he doesn't think anyone would be leaving soon. Placing his arm over Penny's shoulders, he finally asks the question he's been holding back on all evening.

"Okay, Pen. What the hell is bugging you? You were clinging to me like you were afraid I'd leave you alone on the dance floor and you haven't looked me in the eye all night."

"It sounds as though something has gone awry. His tone is one of anger."

"YES, I THINK THERE WILL BE A CHANGE OF PLAN."

Penny's tears began to flow down her cheeks as Don asked his held-back question.

The mention of his leaving her alone brings wails and sobs so loud the window ten inches from theirs is quickly rolled up by the couple in the next car.

"Penny, please stop crying. I'm sorry if I said the wrong thing. Do you have your period, is that what's wrong?"

"No, I *don't* have my period. *That's* what's wrong!"

Don pulls her into his arms but no words were exchanged for a long two minutes while Penny tried to control her sobs. Don didn't know what to say. He was waiting for relief, some word from her that would change what he feared she meant.

When Penny was finally able to talk, her words were not what Don was hoping for.

"You do love me, don't you?"

"Of course, I do."

"Oh Don, what are we going to do?"

"Let's not panic."

He didn't want to question how sure she was, or if tomorrow might bring the relief he wished for, so he took a deep breath and waited. Penny spoke first.

"I'm too upset now to stay here and discuss this. I'm tired. We better go home. We can meet tomorrow."

Don was happy to maneuver the car back onto the road and he hurried to drop Penny off. She leaned over for Don's goodnight kiss as always.

"Call me tomorrow."

The next day, Penny felt sick. Don didn't call and they didn't meet. She called that evening and they had a short discussion.

Penny was unusually calm. "Let's look at all the possibilities." Don was apprehensive but knew the problem had to be faced and listened quietly.

"One. We could consider an abortion. We could both still live at home and go to community college together like we talked about."

Don hadn't planned that far ahead regarding his relationship with Penny, and had applied to schools out of town, and the mention of an abortion brought the sense of relief he so badly wanted.

"True," he replied, hoping that was the end of the conversation.

"Two," Penny went on. It's only been seven weeks since my missed period and I read that sometimes women have miscarriages in the early weeks.

"If that should happen, that would be that."

"Yeah. That would be that."

Don had no idea what she was talking about, but if it meant he was off the hook, he agreed.

"Three, we could get married."

Don sat very still. He did not reply.

Penny asked him to pick her up at her house the next day after school to talk some more before quickly saying good night and "I love you."

"I love you too," came out unbidden from Don's lips.

Penny hung up with no final decision discussed and Don not pressing for one.

Waiting in front of her house the next day, Penny smiled broadly when Don arrived.

"Come on. We have to go in and tell my parents."

"Are you sure you want me to go in with you, Penny? Maybe you better tell them by yourself."

"I'm too scared by myself."

"Why, do you think your father will get violent?"

"Oh, no. My Dad doesn't believe in violence. He really is a very devout preacher.

"I'm just scared to tell him I'm pregnant. I can't count the many times I've heard him say how evil it is to have sex before marriage. But we're in love so it's different."

"I'm not sure your father will understand that."

"I told my Mom last night. She didn't say much, only that abortion was out of the question."

Don gulped. He had an overwhelming feeling of loss. His legs felt weak and he wanted to sit down and absorb what she had said, but Penny was at the door already.

Penny put her house key in the lock. "Anyway she said I had to tell him myself."

She opened the front door and led Don to the den where she knew her father sat every evening reading the newspaper.

Don had been here before, even met her father the night of the prom. There had been a handshake and pictures taken, all quite formal.

Entering the room, he saw Penny's father with his shoulders and head bent standing facing the fireplace.

The preacher's stern look as he turned to them made it obvious that he had already heard the news. Don realized he hadn't seen him wearing his minister's collar before.

"Here comes the fire and brimstone speech."

"What are your plans?" The question was directed to Don, singling him out.

Seeing the panic in Don's eyes, Penny quickly jumped in.

"We're in love and going to get married" she responded, avoiding the word pregnant.

"And how will you support a wife and child?

The question was again directed at Don. Feeling cornered and without time to think, he answered.

"I'll get a job."

"Very well."

Penny was delighted with her father's acceptance and reached to squeeze Don's left hand while her father reached out for his right.

With a handshake from the father/preacher and a 'Welcome to the family' statement that was just as cold as his palm, the plan was quickly sealed shut.

The color in Don's cheeks drained as he suddenly realized what had happened.

Penny's father again directed his glance at Don. "Since you both graduate in two weeks, we'll have a small wedding the following Saturday.

"I'll take care of the church formalities and aside from your parents, it will be private."

"There's no backing out now," thought Don.

The preacher turned his head slightly indicating the meeting was over.

Penny, although relieved, was disappointed that her father had not looked directly at her once.

The guilty feelings welled up inside her.

"We *are* in love, she countered to herself."

They left the den and headed for the front door. Don felt awkward. Suddenly he was embarrassed to hold Penny or seek her lips. He kissed her on the cheek. He was anxious to leave Penny's house and more anxious about going home to break the news.

He knew his parents would be upset and he also naively thought if he didn't say it aloud, it would not be true. He decided to go to his friend Tom's house first. He stopped on the way to get a six-pack.

"You look pretty bad. Come on in." Tom had quit high school two years ago and now had a construction job and an apartment. Don admired him and his independent lifestyle and they remained friends.

A couple of hours later, with his cardboard beer case empty as well as a few more crumpled cans from Tom's fridge on the floor, Don relaxed. He felt the release of tension.

He finally told Tom what was going on.

"Holy shit!" Tom's choice of words struck them both as funny.

"Yeah, that's about what her father was thinking!"

They were both drunk and rolled on the floor laughing at Don's weak attempt at humor.

It was late in the evening when Don went home. His father was at the table.

"About time."

Don's mother quickly changed the subject, knowing that her husband would not stay quiet long.

"I made meat loaf and mashed potatoes with the gravy you like – you know the one with the nice mushrooms."

She urged Don to come to the table. "Sit down and eat, Son."

"I better stand and get what I have to say over with."

His parents were dismayed with the news of the pregnancy, especially when he said, "No getting rid of it. We're going to be married right after graduation. It's all set."

"Well, well. So they're in love. We don't need to analyze their future success. I'll give their marriage a year tops."

"THEY WILL BRING NEW LIFE TO THE WORLD AND THAT MAY STRENGTHEN THEIR UNION."

"Or loosen the slim thread that binds them now."

JAQUAR XK8

ENVY

"C'mon,Moe-reese. You gonna come help or sissy out on us. Shit, you're the only one that drives."

"The prom's over and I'm late already. I shoulda been at my front door now. If my old man's been drinking he's got his belt in his right hand ready to lay stripes on my ass."

"What you got to lose, whippin now or whippin later. If you wait maybe he'll fall asleep. Petey's down the street. He's got his eye on a Jaguar. It'll be easy-peasy – jerk didn't even lock it."

"A Jag? Are you sure? I gotta see this."

Approaching the deep green jaguar, Maurice's ears blot out Mikey's chatter as his eyes take in his dream car. He'd seen the 2004 XK8 model Jaguar once before cruising the neighborhood.

Now he was itching to touch it and get into the tan leather seat and behind the wheel.

"Hurry up guys. What took you so long?

Mikey hurries to squeeze in behind the front seat. Petey's hotwired the car and the engine's humming.

Maurice ignores them both as he slowly slides his open palm lovingly over the chrome plated "Leaper" ornament and then reaches for the door handle. For a moment, he stops to take in the smell of the tan interior and the smoothness of the V8 engine.

He knows the bigger engine was new that year, in fact he knows everything about Jaguars. It's been his ambition to own one as long as he can remember.

The plastic model he got for Christmas ten years ago still hangs from his ceiling on a string held there with a thumb tack. Now here it is for real.

"Sweet." All thought of the forthcoming painful consequences of this moment are quickly wiped away. The wheel feels just right and he handles it gently. He pulls away from the curb slowly, embracing every movement of the jaguar that is now in his control.

Petey's first thought is of music. He reaches over from his seat in front and turns on the radio.

Eminem's "Lose yourself" fills the air and the car starts bouncing in time with Mikey's dance moves in the back seat.

Maurice is still enthralled with his good fortune. "This guy did a great job fixing it up and keeping the interior. That's real wood on the dash."

"I guess the wood's okay but I bet he paid plenty for those speakers.

"Just listen to that bass."

"Hey, Mikey. How about sharing the beer?"

Maurice steps on the brake, slowing his dream car and hoping for the best.

Suddenly the tan leather interior he admired so much turns red and blue as it's lit up by flashing lights and he has to shout to be heard above the siren.

"Stop, Petey. Don't open it. Maybe we can talk our way out. Damn, we only went three blocks."

There was no beating with a strap that night. There was no money for bail either. Maurice's mother cried after his phone call from the police station.

"But I'll be there in the morning. Keep yourself safe son and I'll say a prayer."

She washed away her tears before waking her husband. He was very quiet as she told him, not exploding as she expected him to.

"Damn fool. Well that does it. He won't even graduate high school. I give up, we tried our best." He rolled over in bed.

Not of the same mind, Mrs. Moore wasn't giving up yet. "Our son is not bad, but yes he was foolish. Go back to sleep."

There is no sleep for her.

Often she would stay up watching late night television but each channel she turns to tonight seems to have some story connecting the fate of young blacks to her own son. She fears for his future.

She can't wait any longer. It's now almost dawn. She dials and lets the phone ring four times.

About to hang up, she hears the gravely morning voice of her friend.

"Sadie, I'm sorry. I know it's only six o'clock. Are you awake?"

"I'm awake *now*, Ginny. What's wrong?"

"I need help. Maurice is in jail. The boys took a car for a joy ride. I have to go in to court in a few hours."

"I'm sorry to hear about your boy. I know how upset you are. I've had that same feeling."

"Didn't you tell me that your Jimmy went into the army instead of jail when he got caught shoplifting at Johnson's grocery? How'd he get to do that?"

"Yes, yes. Jimmy's been in the army almost two years. He's in Afghanistan.

"It was Mr. Taylor at the high school that helped him. He was the coach of the basketball team and he went to court with us and spoke to the judge."

"Maybe I can get him to help us, even though Maurice isn't on the team."

"Oh, honey, I'm sorry. He left last year. He went to Ireland or somewhere. Do you need money for bail? I got a little stashed."

"Thank you, no. Money won't help now."

Determined not to fail her son, Mrs. Moore remembered the papers and cards he brought home after an open house night with armed forces sales reps.

They were trying to get kids to join. Maurice had shown no interest but the stuff was still in his trash can.

She called the number on one of the cards and was nervous but relieved to hear a man's voice answering.

"This better be important. It's not even seven o'clock yet."

"Oh, please, don't hang up. I'm desperate. I don't want my son to go to prison. Please help me."

"Whoa. Slow down ma'am. What's the problem?"

Standing in court, Maurice squirmed as his fate was being determined. When the judge admonished him for stealing a car and asked if he would agree to two years in the army instead of jail time he was confused.

One quick look at his mother and he knew it was her doing. The army sergeant standing next to her gave it away.

"Speak up, son. This is your future. It's your choice."

"WELL, ARE YOU GOING TO HELP HIM? YOU PICKED HIM."

"I thought he had potential but now I'm not so sure."

"YOU HAVE BEEN KNOWN TO CHANGE YOUR MIND AS FREQUENTLY AS YOU WILLED THE WIND TO TURN."

"He is big and strong and quite handsome with his brown skin, but he may not be a demi-god after all. This is his time for free will, let's just see how he does."

"YES, AND WE WILL SEE WHAT CHOICE HE MAKES AND WHAT LESSON HE WILL LEARN, IF ANY."

"Yes sir, Judge. I agree."

Maurice does better in the army than Zeus expected, but not as well as God would like.

"I THINK HE HAS WHAT MORTALS CALL A 'CHIP ON HIS SHOULDER.'

"HE SPEAKS OF A 'BUM RAP' FOR JUST TRYING TO HAVE A LITTLE FUN."

"Ha, ha. I see you have picked up the lingo of the mortals but did you give him the old 'thou shalt not steal' or that other hard word, 'covet'?

"YOU JEST AT THE WORDS AS DO THE OTHERS IN HIS GROUP, BUT THEY ALL SEEM BITTER UNDER THEIR LAUGHTER."

"Surely they are bitter. This life is not so different from what they have been used to. Look how they cling to each other – all of them dark skinned. Does this give them a sense of protecting each other against the white army?

"Maurice is bigger and stronger than any of the white soldiers and he wins medals in every competition. Now he has been challenged to single combat in a secret location by one of the white soldiers. When he shows his strength and wins you may then approve of his actions."

"YOU ALSO HAVE LESSONS TO LEARN."

Maurice is sitting on a small stool bent over a large pail grumbling as he uses a sharp knife to peel the skin off a large potato.

"What are *you* complaining about?" Maurice is still ready to fight. His fellow potato peeler is not happy either.

"I would have won if everybody didn't come running to watch and bring the sergeant."

Maurice is quick to reply. "And if I had this knife in my hand then."

"Look at him! He's been reduced to kitchen slave!"

"SO NOW YOU CARE. WHY DID YOU CHANGE YOUR MIND?"

"I find he is a demi-god after all. I remembered Memnon at the siege of troy. He was quite a warrior and he was an Ethiopian King."

"ZEUS, KINGS ARE NOT DEMI-GODS ALTHOUGH I'VE SEEN MANY WHO LIVED BY THAT BELIEF."

"Yes, but Memnon was the son of Eos, the Goddess of Dawn. Maurice should be able to control his actions befitting his station as a demi-god warrior."

"You boys better shut up and keep peeling. I've got to boil those potatoes in an hour and…"

The cook stops talking and does not move. Maurice lifts the knife and his arm stops in mid-air. Zeus is determined to give Maurice a glimpse of history.

Maurice looks over at the other soldier and is amazed to see he's grown a beard and is no longer wearing his uniform. He wonders about the changed color of the tent which looks much smaller and has a sandy floor.

The large pot between his legs seems to have changed shape and has sharp edges. It's now a heavy shield with a drawing of a cross in the middle of it.

He's not scraping it with his knife, but rather is shining it with a scrap of cloth. His boots are laced almost to his knees and he has bands of black leather wound tight on his wrists.

Although he knows this is not his army tent, at the same time he knows that he is in a tent in the huge courtyard of King Priam of Troy's castle.

He's aware he is on a mission to lead an army to fight off the Greeks massed outside the gates of the city.

Preparing to do his duty, he prays to Zeus to help him be victorious.

"AH, BUT HIS PLEA FELL ON YOUR DEAF EARS. YOU WERE COMMITTED TO THE GREEKS DEFEATING AND DESTROYING TROY. SO MEMNON WAS DESTINED TO JOIN THE THOUSANDS OF DEAD WARRIORS BEFORE HE EVEN VENTURED OUT THE GATE."

Zeus is very quiet. His attempt to demonstrate a sense of duty and responsibility to Maurice is now of questionable value.

Maurice blinks a few times before he realizes that the pail is back between his knees.

"What the hell was that? I must have dozed off. Funny, it wasn't a bad dream, more like a bad omen.

"I guess all that Special Forces training crap and our unit getting ready to move out's been on my mind."

Maurice's mother has lots of questions when he calls her to say he might not be in touch for a while.

She asks where he's going and what he'll be doing but he can't tell her. He doesn't know.

The AC-130 transport plane was equipped with heavy machine guns and Maurice noticed a small cannon being loaded as he stepped in.

"Do you know any Muslims?" The seats on the big transport are close together and the young kid buckled in next to Maurice looks a bit pale as he asks.

"We didn't have any in my home town."

Maurice remembered him as the kid getting sharpshooter marks in Basic but they had never spoken.

"There were guys on the block back in New York who changed their names, stopped going to the barber and threw the word Muslim around like it made them righteous."

"There are plenty where we're going. We're part of a group going to train the Syrian Democratic Forces, whoever they are. We have to show them how to handle the newer high powered stuff.

"I hear they don't speak English but there'll be somebody who does at the airport."

"Anybody know which airport?" A voice came from the other side of the plane.

"I saw some papers. Fatisa, or something like that. But I don't know if that was the airport or the town."

Still another voice is heard, "Go to sleep. Who knows when we'll get another chance."

THE MAGIC FLUTE

Abuela Nellis is leaning out the window of the second floor apartment she shares with her son Miguel and her daughter in law Maria to catch the first glimpse of Tayanna.

The bus stop is on Thirtieth Avenue in Astoria, two long city blocks away and she is always relieved when she sees her granddaughter turn the corner.

She worries each day as Tayanna takes a bus from high school to the Performing Arts Center in Flushing for flute lessons and then two buses home. But today is Friday with no flute class scheduled and Tayanna is late.

Placing her elbows further out on the window sill carefully not to crush the morning glories and herbs she likes to grow in the planter, she spots Tayanna. She is dismayed to see that Tayanna is not walking alone.

Abuela came from Mexico for a visit last year and her son would not hear of her going back to live alone. She leaned a little further watching the young man that was walking close to Tayanna toward the house.

She quickly went to the door and stood looking over the hall rail to watch as the boy followed Tayanna up the stairs.

Tayanna is excited and doesn't notice the concerned look on her grandmother's face.

"I have the very best news, Abuela. I got the scholarship to the University I want to go to so badly!"

Abuela stares at the young man and then looks at Tayanna. "Quien es este?" Sensing the tension in her grandmother's voice, Tayanna answers quickly, "Pardon, Abuela. Este es mi amigo de la escuela, Max Alvarez."

"Encantado de conocerte. I am pleased to meet you, Abuela Nellis."

"Bienvenido, Max."

Happy to hear her native tongue, but not quite satisfied, Abuela ushers Max inside and asks, "I know the Ernesto Alvarez family in Cholula, Mexico. Are you any relation?

"No, my family is from Madrid, Spain."

"And you live here now?"

"I live with my mother and my aunt on thirty-ninth. My Spanish is a little different and I make mistakes sometimes but I understand Tayanna.

Still curious, Abuela persists, "And your father?"

"I never knew him.

"He died shortly after my parents married and my Aunt Consuela brought my mother to America to live with her. She was pregnant and I was born right here in Astoria.

"My full name is Maximo, but I like to be called Max."

"Abuela, Max and I want to go to see a movie playing nearby. Maybe he could stay for dinner?" Tayanna's smile is returned. She knew Abuela would never turn a guest away without offering them food.

"Will Mom and Dad be home soon?"

"I don't know. They called and said not to wait dinner. They're at the meeting at CASA in Riverhead.

"It's a long drive, they may be late. I'll start dinner now."

"You have another house in Riverhead?"

"No, Max. The CASA Abuela mentioned is the Center of Alliance, Solidarity and Accompaniment. It's a place dedicated to educating migrant workers about their rights.

"They can learn English and get help with education and immigration. There's never been much support from local government.

"My mother's parents were migrant workers at farms around Riverhead for many generations. My father's grandparents came with a woman who gathered children from small villages and they started working the fields when they were young. It was hard work but a good way to earn money.

"Like my father, I was born in a housing camp on one of the large farms and was carried in a sling on my mother's back until I could walk and follow behind them.

"I learned to dig up potatoes at three and was a full-fledged picker until I was twelve. My father made sure I had books to learn English and math.

"He carved me my first flute from a branch of an aspen tree when I was eight and playing it was a natural fit for me.

"I loved playing music in the fields and it lifted everyone's spirit on those hot days in July and August. They called it my magic flute."

"So how did you get to Astoria?"

"Six years ago my father won a lot of money on the lottery. We had a big party with all our worker friends. We moved to this apartment so I could go to high school here.

It was hard but I soon caught up to my right grade. But don't think we're rich. My father figured out the best way to make it last the longest is not to take it all at once.

"He did buy me the expensive flute I play now and a new television set and I have my own bedroom with nice furniture. Well, I did. Abuela also sleeps in my room now.

"The best is yet to come. My Mom told me in secret that I'm getting a very special graduation present and she hinted at a trip this summer.

"I'd love to backpack around Europe, but I doubt they'd agree to that. More likely it's to Mexico with my Abuela to visit relatives and see where we came from."

"Tayanna," Abuela interrupts, "there's mail for you on the counter and I do want to hear more about the scholarship?"

"It's pretty exciting, a full scholarship to the very best school in the country for the flute. Their students win top prizes and they have excellent teachers."

"That's wonderful, cara mia, but Texas?"

"It's in *North* Texas, Abuela, not too close to the border."

"You're making fun of my fears, but no matter where you are I will pray each night for God to keep you safe."

"Look at this Max. It's from Ancestry.com. This must be my DNA report for the Science Project. Miss Douglas said they'd be mailed home for complete privacy and we can bring them in if we want to. Did you get yours yet?"

"Yes, no surprise there. I'm from Spain and it was ninety-four percent. They even pinpointed an area around Madrid. My Mom said she didn't know it.

"Aunt Consuela explained that the borders of many cities have moved a lot and are different now. She said she didn't remember much from Spain either.

"My mother is an orphan. She gets upset talking about Spain and doesn't like me asking questions about my father. She said only that he was well educated and he was not close to his family."

"Too bad. Do you have any pictures?"

"No, they both told me they left everything behind in Spain."

Abuela tries to comfort the boy. "Hijo, your father's sudden death may have been so hard for your mother that she's blocked all memories of that time in her life."

"I guess so."

Abuela notes the disappointment in Max's eyes and changes the subject.

"Open your letter Tayanna."

"Well I know it will say Mexican like my parents, but I am anxious to read it in print.

"Look, there's a pie chart. Funny, it doesn't say all Mexican. It says forty percent Mexican, forty percent Spanish and twenty percent Aztec.

"Abuela, what does that mean?"

"All that means is that you are truly Mexican. Your blood shows that one or more of your ancestors were the original people, the Aztecs. My grandmother used to talk about the Aztecs and their great civilization."

"Over the years your ancestors married someone from Spain or other parts of Mexico and now with all the mixtures, we are all Mexicans.

"Tayanna, that's so exciting," said Max, smiling broadly. You're also Spanish from Spain, like me!"

"The Spanish part is no great surprise, Max. We pretty much knew the story of the conquistadores from Spain and that there were generations with Spanish blood, but Aztec?

Zeus yawns. ***"This vigil is boring. Tayanna's family is doing good works already and the boy doesn't seem like a would-be hero .We need to spice it up a bit. Light a fire."***

"YES, IT IS TRUE THAT TAYANNA'S PARENTS ARE ALREADY FULFILLING THEIR PROPER ROLE.

"HOWEVER HAVING CHOSEN CHILDREN ABOUT TO BECOME ADULTS CAN HELP US TO SEE IF THEY WILL DO A BETTER JOB TAKING CARE OF THE EARTH.

"TAYANNA AND MAX HAVE TO LEARN WHY THINGS HAVE BECOME THE WAY THEY ARE, WHAT EVENTS MAY HAVE LED TO THE STATUS OF THE WORLD TODAY, AND WHAT THEY MIGHT DO TO EFFECT A CHANGE.

"YOU CAN HOLD OFF ON YOUR LIGHTENING BOLT AND FIRE."

"Forget the movie, Max. Let's get on my computer and look up the Aztecs, my forefathers. The report says I can get more information on line.

Seated at the computer, Tayanna begins reading about a time hundreds of years earlier and is drawn in to the interesting information on the Aztecs.

"In 1345 the Aztec people migrated from an area called Aztlan to Lake Texcoco. They were a Pre-Columbian Mesoamerican people living from the fourteenth to the sixteenth century.

Their capitol city was Tenochtitlan and they built it on a raised island in Lake Texcoco. It later became the site of modern day Mexico City.

"It is said they carried a large statue of a god they worshipped called Huitzilopochtli and they built a pyramid sixty meters high and placed it on a tower…"

Max's cell phone pings, indicating a message and interrupting Tayanna's reading.

"Sorry, my Mom needs me at home. She doesn't feel well and Aunt Consuela isn't there."

"Okay. I'll tell you all about my ancestors at school on Monday.

"I'm going to check out this site. They mention a Museum in Mexico City where they have displays of Aztec artifacts that have been found."

Two hours later, Abuela comes in and finds Tayanna slumped over at her desk making moaning sounds. She gently touches her shoulder. Tayanna jumps up, raising her arms over her head in defense.

"You were dreaming, Cara. Lie down and sleep comfortably in your bed now."

Unable to shake the feeling of fear and not understanding why, Tayanna tries to recall her dream.

"I was dressed in colorful unfamiliar clothes and was serving water to soldiers dressed in really weird clothes with metal breastplates and swords and …Conquistadores!

"That's what they were. Just like the photos on the internet."

"Que?"

"Oh, Abuela, such a dream!

"I was a servant following them on their horses and we came to a big lake and crossed over a bridge to an island with the most beautiful buildings.

"It was like pictures of Venice, Italy, with canals and boats and lots of natives coming to meet the men on horses. We came to a large pyramid and a statue of that god I read about. There were many people gathered together looking up at the statue.

"Most of the men's chests were bare but they were painted and the women wore clothing like mine. They were all chanting softly led by a man in a feathered headdress and markings on his arms and face.

"He looked like a priest in a religious service.

"I heard the most beautiful sounds coming from a flute that a young boy was playing. It was very fancy, with bright gold trim and stones shining in the light of the fires on poles.

"It seemed to me that the boy's music was leading the natives in a prayer. Somehow I understood their words even though it was not the Spanish we speak.

"We thank you Xochipelli for your favors, the flowers of the earth, the beautiful sounds of the music and the love you have shown us."

Tayanna raised her hands to the sides of her head and looked frightened.

"Cara mia, what is it?"

"Oh God, I remember it all now.

"The horse in front of me started rearing up as the conquistador urged him forward.

"Three of the other horses were prodded and a panic broke out in the group of natives as the soldiers raised their swords and raced at them.

"I saw one of the conquistadores gallop quickly and kill the priest and another dismount and attack the boy, grabbing the lovely carved flute. I saw it plainly as he rode away.

"It was covered with the boy's blood."

MEXICO CITY

"Abuela, look around."

Tayanna's grandmother grew up in rural Mexico with the fear of the 'big city' part of her culture. As promised she has accompanied Tayanna to Mexico for a vacation before she begins her studies at the University of North Texas and is nervous today in Mexico City.

"The buildings are beautiful and so interesting," Tayanna assures her. "I'm sure it's safe and after we visit the museum we'll go to visit your cousin in Puebla."

Located within the grounds of Chapultepec Park, the lovely landscaped courtyard of the National Museum of Anthropology invites them in. The walkway frames a large water feature with exhibits and statues among the shrubs surrounding the main building.

Tayanna and her grandmother hear the guide as they enter. They decide to follow along as she leads a small group through the museum.

"The museum features many artifacts from Aztec, Mayan and Toltec cultures including stone carvings, Aztec goddess statues, and one of my favorites, the Sun Stone."

The group stops as she describes the intricate designs on the Aztec Calendar Stone in the Mexica Hall.

"The large stone is three feet deep and almost twelve feet wide in diameter. It has been placed upright on a stone pedestal here but would have been flat on the ground and was part of the Temple Mayor complex.

"We believe it dates back to the 1400's. Different theories have been put forth about the central figure. It may represent the Day Sun, the Night Sun, or some say the primordial earth monster, Tlaltecuhtli, representing the final destruction of the world as the fifth sun falls.

The adults in the tour group stare in wonder at the face in the center of the Stone and some of the children make faces in imitation. Abuela listens intently, remembering stories of the Aztec Gods from her childhood. She had thought of them as myths.

Zeus has not been interested in the trip to Mexico so far but the Sun Stone gets his attention.

"This event is finally becoming interesting."

"The four eras of the Suns- the Jaguar, the Wind, the Rain of Fire, and Water- those are the faces you see surrounding the center.

"They succeeded each other after the gods Quetzalcoatl and Tezcatlipoca struggled for control of the cosmos until the era of the present fifth sun.

"We are now considered to be in that fifth sun era and the ancient prediction was that the era of the Earthquake will be the next one.

"Antonio de Leon y Gama, an astronomer became the first scholar to understand the system represented in the Calendar Stone. He claimed that the Aztecs in their observations of the heavens had been on the same cultural level as the great civilizations of ancient Greece and Egypt."

"By the stars, now that is most interesting. The Stone tells the story of their existence, much like what has been called the myth of the Olympian Gods.

"I have often referred to the Age of Gaia, the Age of Uranus and the Age of my Titan father, Cronos. Perhaps I myself was the God who brought the earthquake of destruction to my realm."

"YOU GIVE YOURSELF TOO MUCH CREDIT. THE PEOPLE YOU RULED LIVE AND PROSPER TODAY AS DO THE AZTECS AND MAYANS. OF COURSE THEY NOW RULE THEMSELVES.

"THIS WAS ANOTHER EXAMPLE OF THE DESTRUCTION OF A CIVILIZATION BECAUSE IT WAS MISUNDERSTOOD AND ITS VALUE TO THE WORLD UNDERESTIMATED. IT IS ALL TOO CLEAR IN THE HINDSIGHT OF MAN."

The tour guide continues, "We know that at some time after the Spanish Conquest, the stone was buried in the Zocalo, our main square.

"It was found in 1792 during repairs of the Mexico City Cathedral and was mounted on a wall of the Cathedral until 1885 when it was brought here."

Abuela smiles at the Sun Stone, proud that it is an important part of her family heritage. The myths were now real to her.

Here in front of her was something solid she could see with her own eyes. She had a warm feeling of belonging as she looked around at historic pieces from the lives of her own ancestors.

The group moves on to sculptures and pottery and then they spread out around a small scale model of the ancient Aztec capital of Tenochtitlan.

Tayanna makes her way to the front of the group. She feels dazed and leans on the arm of her grandmother as the scene she remembers from her dream unfolds before her eyes.

Every detail comes flashing back - the temple, the religious ceremony, the menacing yells of the charging Conquistadors, the smell of their sweating horses, the chaos and the boy with the golden flute. Only now she doesn't remember the blood as her mind concentrates on the clear lovely sounds of the flute.

"What is it, my child. You look pale. You didn't eat enough this morning. Let's have a cup of tea and some biscochitos."

"Was that you or my brother Hades trying to frighten her? What effect can she possibly have on what happened so long ago?"

"THE SMALL ACTIONS, EITHER GOOD OR EVIL, OF ONE MORTAL TODAY WILL HAVE AN EFFECT ON TOMORROW."

Tayanna shudders and decides not to worry Abuela who is already nervous in Mexico so she agrees and they head to the museum restaurant as she tries to understand her daydream.

"I feel that I've been sent a message from the past about that little boy and his flute. His music came to me for a reason. I know he needs my help."

At the hotel that evening, Tayanna puts a photo she has taken of the Aztec Sun Stone on Instagram.

A few minutes later she receives a message from Max saying that he wishes he was there with her.

"I wish you were too," she quickly messages back. "It was real creepy at the museum."

Moments later, Tayanna's cell phone plays a few familiar notes and she knows from the ring that Max is calling.

"Are you okay, Tayanna? You seemed frightened in your text."

"I'm okay, but I need to tell someone what happened at the museum today and I don't want to frighten Abuela. Thanks for calling.

"Remember my dream about the Conquistadores the day I found out about my Aztec blood?

"Well, I swear that I could hear that flute playing and see what happened in my dream all over again right there in the Mexica Hall."

"What do you think it all means?"

"I believe that the flute truly belongs right here in Mexico City and I wish I knew what happened to it."

"Tayanna, it may be just a coincidence but I found something interesting today at the library. Since you were in Mexico I looked for books on the Mayan Civilization and found out about the Dresden Codex book.

"It's not really a book, more like a long strip of drawings.

"It's real old, thirteenth or fourteenth century and was done on amate paper which is like bark from a tree. The hieroglyphic art shows scenes with pottery, and there are murals, some depicting images of people playing the flute. And listen to this – Template 34 of the Codex associates the flute with religious rituals."

"You just gave me goose bumps. Now I really have to find that flute."

Zeus smiles, remembering the times he had been entranced with the sounds of Pan's flute.

"This afternoon Abuela insisted on going on to the Cathedral to see where the Sun Stone had been found and had hung for so long. We met an interesting old priest there, Father Gabriel, who told us more about the meaning of the Stone.

"I didn't tell him about my dream. He would have thought I was nuts, but I asked what would have happened to some of the things from the temple.

"He said that many things were sent to Spain. Max, we must keep looking for information on Conquistadors. Maybe one of them took the flute back to Spain."

"That could just work out. My Aunt Consuela's talking about a trip to Spain. My mother's not feeling well right now, but she and Consuela have been making plans and I'm sure they include me even though they whisper a lot."

"That trip sounds pretty exciting. Maybe you can find out more about your father and your Mom might remember more when she's there.

"I hope so. It's all such a mystery and my mother still gets upset when I question her about him."

"Father Miguel told us about the monastery of La Asuncion Cuernavaca. He said it was the fifth of fourteen monasteries that were built after the arrival of the Spanish in 1519.

"They held Christian services hoping they could persuade the natives to change their beliefs. It worked well although artifacts survived and ceremonies of the Mayans and Aztecs are still remembered and honored.

"Father Miguel told us about the twelve friars who arrived in Mexico in 1524 and said that much of the population had died of the smallpox introduced from

Europe and one of the Franciscan missionaries studied the people and wrote about their culture.

"I guess the superstition surrounding the Sun Stone is getting to me – a new era can come at any time wiping away the present one.

Remember that news story about the Mexican volcano that erupted last month. It's called Popocatepetl and there was a plume of ashes that went up over 6,000 feet. It's happened many times before and people say it will no doubt happen again."

"The Popocateptl volcano is near the monastery Faher Miguel told us about and my Abuela won't go anywhere near it."

"The child speaks of the Stone of theAztec Gods and the superstitions of the people and her thoughts bring revelations of dire predictions.

"What explanation do you have for this volcano phenomenon? Perhaps there was a flaw in your creation, or was it an intended weakness to test endurance.

"What are your thoughts on the state of the world now and what are your plans?"

Zeus expects no answer and gets none.

MADRID

Seventy-Eight year old Don Alejandro Garcia takes the letter handed to him on a tray by his long time valet, Juan. Don Alejandro is the head of an upper class family that was once part of the royal family of Spain. Since his grandfather's time, they have not been considered royalty but he continues to use the title, Don. He maintains a large estate and is a proud man.

The youngest of his sons, Emilio, is a Catholic priest serving at the Cathedral in Madrid. It is not unusual for the second son to choose the priesthood when the first son has been groomed to take over the family fortune and responsibilities of the father as indeed Emilio's older brother Alvaro has.

Alvaro is now an officer in the Spanish army. He attended the elite Spanish Military Academy in Zaragoza as many young aristocrats have before him.

Don Alejandro was pleased when Alejandro was assigned to NATO's Resolute Support Mission earlier this year to cooperate, support and advise in Afghanistan.

Spain has sent many troops to Afghanistan in support of NATO and Don Alejandro feels it is proper for his eldest son to do his duty.

"A letter for you from America, Sir." The valet's eyes are lowered as usual but there is a knowing glimmer in them.

"Thank you, Juan." He glances at the envelope and lays it aside on the small table next to his glass of Madeira wine, waiting to open it after Juan has left the room.

There has been a good relationship between the men for over twenty years, but it has always been confined to simple conversations between employer and servant.

Juan had noticed the name of the sender on the envelope. He thought he could smell her sweet perfume as he carried it, although he knew it was not likely. America is a long way from Spain and the odor of the mail bag would have taken over. It was his memory that fooled his nose.

At the age of fifteen, Juan had entered service at the Garcia estate. Two years had passed when a young girl of sixteen named Consuela joined the staff and captured his heart.

There was no time in the busy household for long conversations, but Juan managed a few words and soon they were spending rare days off together walking in the garden getting to know each other.

Consuela was hired to care for the infant Emilio, a son born to Don Alejandro's wife Dona Emilia.

The pregnancy had been difficult and she was still bedridden with a nurse caring for her. Her illness was severe and the care of the newborn fell to Consuela.

Don Alejandro rarely visited the nursery and looked disturbed when he did. He spent many hours at the bedside of his wife and in consultation with her doctors.

Her death on the eve of Emilio's second birthday brought great sadness to Don Alejandro and had a serious effect on his feelings for the boy. The day he was born Don Alejandro was happy to name him Emilio after his mother, now the name stuck in his throat and he never used it.

Emilio's hair was blonde like his mother's. He had the same green eyes and pale skin. His smile was hauntingly like hers. In Don Alejandro's mind, the baby had taken the life of his beloved wife and he avoided seeing the child as much as possible.

Their first son Alvaro was ten years old. He did not require assistance but much to Consuela's consternation, he spent his time at home following her around and telling her how much he adored her.

Juan was amused and told her that the young boy would soon tire of his flirting and move on to someone else.

However Alvaro's flirtations persisted for some time and Consuela tried to avoid him. She was relieved when he was enrolled in a prestigious boarding school and was only present during the holidays and summer vacation.

Juan and Consuela's attraction grew, but they were aware that the rules of the household forbid any personal relationships and they were still quite young. They agreed that when Emilio was sent to school at the age of six, she would no longer be needed and would find another job and they could explore their feelings at that time.

In the summer of his fifth year Emilio had become a bit harder to handle. His older brother was often home on weekends and seemed to stir mischief in the boy and in the rest of the household. It was past time for bed and Consuela went to the kitchen in search of her charge since he often begged for sweets or took them when no one was looking.

She heard Don Alejandro yelling loudly at his son Alvaro. She recognized the kitchen maid Maria who was crying softly in the corner. No one else was in the room.

Consuela had heard whispers of a love affair in the kitchen but had kept her thoughts to herself about it.

In the morning Don Alejandro called Consuela to the library. Maria was sitting quietly and she was directed to a chair as well.

Without mentioning his son's name, he spoke of Maria needing help.

"She is pregnant and since she came to us from an orphanage and does not wish to have her child born there, I must see to her well being. You have been doing a good job and are quite capable of caring for her and the child and that would be a huge help to Maria, and to me."

While he was speaking he took a check book lying on his desk and started writing in it.

He ripped a check out of the book and with a flourish presented it to Consuela.

"I would like you to continue working for me, Consuela, however it would be in America.

Consuela was taken aback in surprise and about to object, but her eyes grew wide as she saw the amount of the check he was handing her.

It was more than a year's salary. Thoughts of what that much money meant leapt to her mind. "Juan could quit and join me in America."

"But," she said, "Don Alejandro, what about Emilio? Who will care for him?

"That is no longer your concern. He will leave for school a bit earlier than was expected."

Consuela feels sad for young Emilio.

She is fond of the child she has cared for and starts to speak but Don Alejandro quickly goes back to the crisis at hand.

"All living expenses for both you and Maria will be taken care of. I will inform the staff of your decision to go to America on your own. No mention will be made of Maria who has already quit."

Arrangements had been made for a flight to New York City leaving the next day as well as someone to meet them at the airport and make living arrangements.

It was clear that her position at the estate was at an end and she would now be taking care of Maria and the child that Don Alejandro would not acknowledge.

That evening Consuela told Juan the news that she was going to America with the young maid who was pregnant and would write as soon as she was settled. She showed him the check with a big smile on her face.

Although he did not want Consuela to go, he realized it was an opportunity to begin their life together.

Juan said nothing to others of their plans or what he knew of Maria and Alvaro, but the talk took a bad turn and the whispering went on.

Somehow the gossipers had determined that Consuela had left because she was pregnant.

No one dared mention any name with regard to the father, but Alvaro was sent back to school before summer vacation ended and did not come home for the winter holiday that year.

The gossipers spread their version of the events. Although he knew there was no truth to the rumors, as the years went by with no word from Consuela, Juan too had doubts.

Now the letter on the side table burned in Juan's mind. The one time he had asked Don Alejandro for an address to write to Consuela, he was told she did not want it to be given out.

He did not know that Consuela had written and that her letters had been destroyed.

Consuela was told that Juan had left the estate and that there would be no further contact with anyone in the household. Both believed the other was no longer interested in them.

There was much disappointment and each of them had chosen to avoid opening their hearts again.

That was over twenty years ago. There had been no word, but now there was a letter.

Juan's heart had been broken then, now he was just curious.

Don Alejandro is also curious.

"She must want more money," he thought as he stared at the envelope.

"Why else would she write now? My banker has taken care of everything and I have been quite generous."

He went to his desk, picked up his silver initialed letter opener and slit the letter open.

"Dear Don Alejandro,

It will no longer be necessary for you to remit money for your grandson. The trust that was set up will now be turned over to him. He is a capable twenty year old man and has been taught how to handle his finances.

I have told him nothing of his family. He believes his father to be deceased. However we have plans to visit Madrid soon and he may well seek answers to questions his mother and I have avoided. Unfortunately she passed away recently after a long illness.

He believes his name to be Maximilian Alvarez, one his mother chose and insisted on. I have suggested he search the church records knowing there are none to be found.

Please also accept my notice since my services will not be needed.

Your faithful former employee, Consuela."

QUEENS CENTER MALL

"This place is a wonder. It is a palace filled with every imaginable dream of riches. The marble floors rival those on Olympus and you can see right through the walls."

"YES, YES I KNOW. IT'S A GATHERING PLACE TO EAT, DRINK AND SOCIALIZE WITH ALL MANNER OF DESIRABLE OBJECTS AROUND YOU. "IT IS HARD TO UNDERSTAND SINCE I HAVE SOMETIMES HEARD IT REFERRED TO AS A TEMPLE.

"I RESERVE MY THOUGHTS ON THE SUBJECT. LET'S JUST FOLLOW THE ONES WE ARE HERE TO WATCH."

Zeus, as usual, is most interested in following the movements of Athena, who is in the mall today with her friend Judith.

"That dress was fabulous. It really looked good on you, Athena. Red's your color with your dark hair."

"It was fun to try on, Judith, but it isn't in my budget because I'm saving every penny for school.

"Let's get going. I've got to work at the diner. My brother wants to go to a basketball game and I have to clear tables for him."

"I'm sorry for you. I'm glad *I* don't have to work. My trust fund should see me through college and half my life after that."

Judith Tucker was orphaned when she was seven years old. Riding in the back seat of the family Cadillac that was moving quickly along on the Long Island Expressway, she lost consciousness when a truck on their right swerved and the impact sent their car into oncoming traffic.

She doesn't remember the details of the crash that took the lives of her parents and her mind has shut tightly on the subject.

What she does remember is Jesus being there. He looked just like the pictures in her Sunday school lesson book with his arms outstretched to save her.

She didn't realize it was a fireman. The only picture in her mind was Jesus lifting her carefully and pulling her away from the mangled car. When she opened her eyes in the hospital it was the only memory she had of the accident.

Her mother's parents had flown in from their home in Alaska. Judith had only seen them once when she was a toddler.

They did come to the hospital to see her but could only think of the loss of their daughter and left abruptly before she regained consciousness.

Judith was still in the hospital and did not attend the funeral. Details of her parents' deaths were kept to a minimum by everyone around her and she didn't ask any questions.

Although her grandparents worried at first about her lack of concern at the loss of her parents, they accepted the psychologist's remarks that she was shielding her grief by blocking out memory of the accident, even of her life with her mother and father.

In Judith's mind, her parents were whisked away by some unknown force and were not really dead, just gone.

The dramatic change in Judith's life had come to her suddenly.

Her family had been on their way to Astoria from their home in Bridgehampton further out on Long Island for Grandma Tucker's Thanksgiving Dinner.

Judith had always looked forward to visits there. The house was much smaller and there were no maids, but Grandma's cooking was welcome and Grandpa was always available to play games.

The Tuckers were devastated and did not want to pass the weight of their grief for their son and daughter in law onto the child.

They thought it best to start her new life with them in a cheerful atmosphere and rarely mentioned the past.

The guest room she had often stayed in overnight was newly decorated in the pink and lavender Judith preferred and all new clothing and toys were carefully placed in the closet and dresser drawers.

Judith considered the Christmas held at the Tuckers that year the best one ever. Every single thing on her list was under the tall blue spruce decorated with sparkling lights and many small crosses and Jesus figurines that she had chosen herself.

She attended the small Presbyterian Church with her grandparents on Sundays and prayed every night before bed, always thanking Jesus for saving her life.

She preferred the Christian television station to the Disney Channel and as a teenager even to iTunes and You Tube on her cell phone. There was no objection when she wanted to attend the Christian Church of Astoria but the Tuckers insisted on public high school.

When she was teamed up with Athena Pappas for a high school project and Athena willingly did all the work and shared the credit, Judith found she had a friend.

The Tuckers were named as legal guardians. Grandfather Tucker set up a trust for Judith with the proceeds of the two million dollar house in Bridgehampton and the insurance monies.

"Hey I'm not complaining about working, Judith. I get ten bucks an hour working for my father at the diner and I can use that experience to find a job waitressing when I'm at nursing school in the fall.

"The great rice pudding my father makes and all I can eat fries is just a bonus.

"And you, my friend, can just sit there with all your money and give me big tips while I wait on you. You're still going to be my room-mate aren't you?"

"I do enjoy being waited on, but I'm not up for waiting on anyone myself, so nursing is out for me. "I'm thinking of something like astronomy.

It sounds easy and there's this really cute geek in my science class. He's going to Texas A&M for astronomy."

"Texas A&M may be in the same state, but I thought you were going to Texas Women's with me

"Don't desert me now. I hope you're still my best friend and I need my best friend close by, in my room to be exact."

"Stop worrying. My trust will pay for a lot of tips and I'm planning on getting a car, so we can travel in style in Texas. Maybe even to Texas A&M.

"And yes, I'm going to be your room-mate. I was just teasing. Hope you don't mind a large screen television and Google Home for our music."

Judith stops talking and grabs Athena's arm pulling her to the window of the Baby Gap store.

"What's up with you, that hurt and why are we looking at stuff for little kids?"

"Look over your shoulder at the two guys coming out of the Verizon store.

"There's that guy I told you about from my science class, the good looking one."

"He looks familiar. I think he goes to my church. Yeah, I saw him last Sunday. He pretty much keeps to himself, but he did stop me and asked if I went to Townsend Harris.

"He surprised me and I choked up and couldn't think of anything more than my name to say, but I smiled and said yes about school. He just blushed and walked away. That was it. His name's Michael Poulos."

Bill Parker and Michael have been friends since grammar school. Their interests differ but they often ride their bikes to the library together.

Michael always heads for the desk to see if any new books have come in on space travel and Bill checks out mystery novels.

They're at the Mall today hoping to secure jobs for the summer. Bill got lucky at the Food Court.

One cook he spoke to noticed he looked Asian and liked his reference to his Vietnamese grandmother. He told Bill to come back the next day when the manager would be there.

Michael was making the rounds of shops but has had no offers. He spots Athena and feels the urge to talk to her again.

"There's that Greek girl I know from school and church, the girl with the dark hair.

"I think I know her friend from my science class. She stares at me a lot, but I usually ignore her. Let's go over."

"Okay by me. The red head's real cute."

"Athena, walk slowly. He's looking this way."

"Are you that interested?"

"I could be. Anyway they're coming over. Here's my chance."

"Hi, Athena. Remember me, Michael?"

"Sure. Michael, this is my friend Judith."

"Hi Judith. I think you were in my science class. This is my friend Bill. Would you both like to get a coke at the Food Court?"

Judith jumped at the chance to spend time with Michael. "Sure, we'd love to. I'm really thirsty and I bet Athena is too."

"I'm sorry. I am thirsty, but I'm on my way to work and I have to go. But you go ahead. Judith, I'll see you tomorrow."

Judith is disappointed but quickly turns her frown at Athena into a smile in Michael's direction.

"Okay, why don't we…"

But Michael has already turned away from her and is talking to Athena. "I've been looking for a job. Where do you work? Any hope for me there?"

"Hard to say, but we can usually use another dishwasher. It's my Dad's diner. I can ask."

"Better yet, why don't I go with you and ask your father in Greek. That might work."

Bill, realizes it's a good chance to be alone and get to know Judith.

"Come on, Judith. We can still get a coke or something."

Not sure if she wants to ditch this friend of her dream guy, Judith smiles at Bill. "Okay, sure. Are you and Michael close friends?"

"Sort of. You were in his science class, weren't you?

"He really lives and breathes that stuff. It's kinda boring to me."

"So he did remember me," thought Judith.

"THE CHILD JUDITH NEEDS LOVE AND COMPASSION. SHE PUSHES ASIDE HER DEEP FEELINGS OF LOSS AND FILLS HER NEED WITH THINGS THAT HER MONEY CAN BUY."

"Unfortunately, it looks like young Michael is more attracted to"…about to say 'my Athena,' Zeus catches himself. ***… "the girl Athena."***

There is no comment made by God, but he's watching and notices that Michael is following the plan and staying close to Athena.

It's some weeks after the day Michael went with Athena to her father's diner and asked for a job.

"George, can you cover for me. Michael's off work soon and he's invited me to go to the Planetarium.

"Yeah, okay Sis, but what's with that guy. If it was me, I'd take you to a movie."

"I kind of agree with you, but I like him even though he's a geek. He's unique.

"Like when he spoke Greek to Pop and discussed mythology and how the Greeks named the stars.

"He knew some story of Atlas spinning the globe on his shoulders to keep the stars rising and setting. Then Pop smiled and hired him on the spot."

Zeus is not pleased that Athena is impressed with Michael.

"He's not so unique. Why I myself placed Aex, the daughter of Helius the Sun in the sky as Capricorn. And I rewarded the goat whose milk I drank as an infant.

"You can see her and the two baby goats in the constellation Auriga."

"I RECALL THE EGYPTIANS USING THE STARS BEFORE YOU FOR MORE PRACTICAL PURPOSES LIKE TO DETERMINE THE TIME OF THE NILE RIVER FLOODING."

Their thoughts are interrupted as the door leading to the kitchen swings open and Michael's head appears.

"I'll be finished in a minute, Athena. Breakfast dishes are done, just wiping up."

George smiles as the door shuts. "He's a good worker even if he's geeky. Have a good time."

As they're about to leave the diner, Soft chimes ring on Athena's cell phone and she answers Judith's text explaining that she and Michael are going to the planetarium.

Judith returns a text, "Wait for me. I'm almost there. Michael hasn't seen my new car."

Judith pulls up in front of the diner in her new lime green Jeep Wrangler five minutes later."

"Michael, how do you like my new car?"

"It's okay. What's with the button?

Judith's white tank top has a two inch round clip on button with President Trump's face covered with his slogan, "Make America Great."

"Our youth group at church is gearing up for the November elections. We want to be sure Trump stays in office and Congress needs to keep the Republicans in charge.

"We're making headway – ditching Roe v. Wade is next."

"Judith, you don't really think that, do you? I mean, like free choice and all that goes with it."

Shrugging her shoulders, Judith comments, "Yeah, I know. You would have voted for Hilary, but all I know is my trust fund is getting bigger every day."

Michael quickly defuses the conversation. "Your car looks great, Judith."

"I'm especially excited that we'll have it at school. You know your university and ours are just three hours apart."

"Sounds good, Judith. You two can visit Bill and me often. We're sharing a dorm room. It'll be fun."

"Well, let's go to the Planetarium today. Maybe we can go for a long drive out on the island soon and you can take the wheel.

"Come on now, sit up front. I can show you all the upgrades."

"THAT'S A GOOD SIGN. MICHAEL SEEMS TO BE A PEACEMAKER.

"He's okay. He stays close to Athena, but perhaps Judith is more suited to the boy."

Zeus tries again not to disclose his keen interest in Athena and God feels assured that Michael will continue his involvement with her.

Michael accepts Judith's invitation to sit in the front seat next to her, but during the drive he constantly turns back to include Athena in the conversation.

"I'm really excited to show you the Space Show and there's a program today called "Astronomy Live: The Perfect Planet."

Judith remarks, "Sounds like a Star Trek movie."

Michael smiles at Judith but quickly returns to addressing his comments to Athena.

"You'll enjoy the Space Show. It's a large theater that is actually in the top half of Planetarium Sphere. It has the largest vertical reality simulators. It's a 3-D map of the universe with the planets, star clusters, nebulae and galaxies and it makes you feel like you're in a space ship floating out there.

"Sounds like a pleasant dream." Athena leans forward, closer to Michael.

"Yes, it's a dream I have quite often."

EYE IN THE SKY

Michael and Bill settled into their shared dorm room at Texas A&M. Almost immediately, Judith showed up there in her lime green jeep. At first Athena grudgingly accompanied her, not wanting to take time away from her studies, but she soon found that she did enjoy Michael's company and the trips took place often.

When he flew home from Texas A&M on his first Spring Break, Bill Parker's Dad drew him aside on Easter Sunday and asked him to go to spend a few days with his grandparents in West Virginia before going back to school.

"We haven't gone since they moved there six years ago and you can tell them all about college. They'd be happy to see you."

Although he had heard his Mom and Dad argue and his mother had never said so to him, he knew she didn't get along with Dad's mother and probably didn't want him to go.

Bill quickly agreed but kept thinking about it afterward.

"I think Dad feels like I'll make up for his not seeing them more often.

"Mom didn't say much to me, but I've heard her refer to Grandma as a "G.I. Bride" a couple of times. To me she's just Grandma.

One time when Bill asked his Mother about the first time she met Father's family, she started to cry and said that her uncle had been killed in Viet Nam.

She had heard terrible stories about the war from her mother. So when she met the Vietnamese woman who would be her mother in law, she was upset and very disappointed.

Bill has always felt comfortable with his grandmother, mostly because he resembles her so much. His mother often joked that his looks were just an unlucky draw of the cards. His father didn't smile and when Bill was young always gave him a hug after that remark.

"It is rare to find a cold heart in a mother."

"YOU ARE RIGHT. IT IS ALSO RARE TO RESENT YOUR CHILD BECAUSE HE DOES NOT FAVOR YOUR FEATURES AND SKIN COLOR. MANY ADOPTED CHILDREN ARE ACCEPTED LOVINGLY BY PARENTS WHOSE SKIN MAY BE DIFFERENT FROM THEIRS.

"THE BOY SEEMS TO HAVE GROWN UP UNSCATHED. HIS GRANDMOTHER MAY HAVE CONTRIBUTED THE MOTHER LOVE THAT HE NEEDED AS AN INFANT."

It was a seven hour drive to Franklin, West Virginia in the Shenandoah Valley. Bill's on Route 33 and decides to stop for gas in Harrisonburg, Virginia before getting ready to go over the mountain range to enter West Virginia.

Spotting a Super Walmart sign just off I-81, he remembers his Dad telling him to bring some flowers for his grandmother.

He smelled the fresh baked goods when he walked in and decided to pick up an apple pie too. It was his favorite and he remembered it was Grandfather Parker's as well.

The last hour of the drive is a new experience for him. Growing up in Astoria and spending most of his free time on the beaches of Long Island didn't prepare him for the breathtaking views and narrow curves of the road as he drove up the mountain range out of Virginia and down into West Virginia.

"YOU ARE UNUSUALLY QUIET."

"The beauty reminds me of my home."

"MAJESTIC MOUNTAINS REACHING UPWARD GIVE ME A WARM FEELING TOO."

The "Watch for Falling Rocks" sign brings a smile to Bill's lips since he cannot fathom the severity of such an event. He turns on the GPS as the road levels out and notices that many of the houses are built with some stone. It makes him think of the big difference to the cement surroundings he's used to.

Franklin is a small town and the GPS leads him right to their hilly driveway in a few minutes.

There's a small wooden porch and Grandma is sitting in a rocker, waiting. She looks patient, but tired. He's reminded of how much he looks like her with the darker skin tone, black hair and slanted eyes.

Her dark eyes light up and she smiles as he hands her the small bouquet of flowers

She hugs Bill and the top of her head barely reaches his shoulders. The screen door creaks as Grandfather joins them.

His handshake is tight. "Welcome."

"Hope you like apple pie."

"My favorite."

"Look how tall he's grown, Papa. Maybe even an inch or two over you." Grandmother beams at both of them standing together.

When they enter the front room, Bill admires the new art work filling every wall.

There are unframed canvasses of various sizes filled with scenes of a small village. One has children playing in a field while women with peaked hats shading their faces work around them.

Another has an older man in a similar hat pushing a small plow. There is a large one with an indoor setting and a woman sitting at a small wooden table chopping vegetables. A young girl sits beside her, watching.

"These are your grandmother's childhood memories from before the war. She had no time to pack photographs when we left Viet Nam. Since we moved here to this quiet isolated community, she spends many hours painting.

“The first time I saw her she was sitting on a bench outside her house sketching on a board with a piece of charcoal. She wasn’t painting the war around her, but a bird in the tree nearby. She was beautiful and it was love at first sight, as they say in the movies.

“It was difficult for us to get married in Viet Nam, but we managed to get out in time.

The look on his face went from one of admiration of his wife to one of bitterness.

“I didn’t know then what awaited us in the States or even in my own home. Neither one of us have been given the respect we deserve.”

“Not now, Papa. The boy has come to have a good time. No need to bring up the past. You can take him for a ride after dinner. Not much to see here.

“Maybe take him over to Sugar Grove. That’s interesting.”

“Do you know how to handle a rifle?”

Surprised at Grandfather’s question, Bill shook his head from side to side.

“Well, I was planning to hunt squirrel tomorrow if you’re interested in joining me.”

“Is that in the sugar grove that Grandma mentioned?”

“No, no. Sugar Grove is another story. It’s a town near here. I met an old Navy guy at the vet center and he told me all about it. He was one of the six families that moved into government housing there around October of 1967. It was a Naval Information Center Support Base.

I lived in WV in 1967 and I remember this place

"He said his wife loved the nice new two story townhouse and the five Navy wives were very friendly. She complained though about it being a National Radio Quiet Zone and there was no television."

"Get to the interesting part, Papa."

"Well, as my buddy tells me, there were two areas to the base. One area was where the five families and two officer's wives lived and the other was an underground facility in a secluded area in the mountains.

"He remembered the rigorous interrogation he went through for his high security clearance.

"There was a special antenna built in the secluded area to capture signals from the satellites orbiting at that time, mostly looking for Soviet messages. Some of the newspaper articles called it the "Big Ear."

"Wow, this I gotta see. Can we go tomorrow?"

"Slow down. We can see the present day town of Sugar Grove which the government recently sold and is being made over into a substance abuse center.

"However, the other part is in the hands of the National Security Agency with their agents operating it now and there's a heavily restricted entrance.

"I would like to see it myself and I often wonder who they're listening to now but doubt we'd get in.

"Come on outside Bill and let me show you how to handle a rifle. These days you never know when you might need to defend yourself or at least shoot an animal to feed your family.

LOVE UNDER FIRE

"The lunch you packed was okay, Penny. I had the peanut butter and jelly sandwiches and I gave Jonesy the foreman the chocolate chip cookies. He's been good to me. Gives me a lot of tips at work, even showed me how to use some of the power tools."

"Sounds good, Hon, but I'm so tired I can't keep my eyes open. Can you please feed Donny now and do the two o'clock feeding tonight. I just have to get a good eight hours sleep. The bottles are all set in the fridge. Just heat them up in the pot of water on the hot plate."

Penny heads for the couch to lie down. She moves aside the pile of clean laundry to make room.

"I'll fold these tomorrow."

"Why don't you ask my Mom to help, Pen? I know she wouldn't mind."

"No, it's enough they let us have this place in their basement for very little rent. We said we'd do this on our own and we will.

"Maybe when Donny's a year old we'll be able to find a sitter, and I can go to work.

"Right now, I just need to sleep."

Don opens the mini-fridge that was meant to go to college with him, unscrews the top on a bottle of beer and takes a sip.

"You may as well go to bed now. I'll put in my ear plugs and listen to the radio while I study."

"And do the two o'clock?"

"Yes, Penny, I'll do the two o'clock. You just put him to sleep in his crib now."

"THEY SEEM TO BE HANDLING THE COMPLEXITIES OF A NEW LIFE WELL. IT IS A DIFFICULT TASK FOR THOSE SO YOUNG."

"I agree that raising babies is difficult, but more interesting are Don's frequent visits with his friend Tom. They often finish a couple of six packs watching Monday night football games and he likes to stop for a beer with the guys after work.

"Let's see how he does tomorrow. Penny told him she intends to stay home with Donny until he's a year old."

"Mr. Jones, I really need a raise. Penny is not quite ready to leave the baby and go to work."

"I understand you need more money, Don, but it's just not possible. Now if you were licensed, instead of just a laborer, I could do something for you. It means studying and passing an exam, but I think you can do it."

Don was pleased at his supervisor's response to his request for a raise and Penny was happy.

"With you making more money, we can get our own apartment."

"Maybe, but I have to study to pass the test first. Can't you stop the baby's crying? Stick a binky in his mouth or something."

"I'm sorry. Donny's just not an easy baby. He's eating every two hours instead of four like the book says and he doesn't sleep very long in between."

"Well, his crying won't pay the rent on an apartment. Without you working, we need more from me or we'll be staying right here in the basement."

"Isn't it odd that the father never refers to his son by his name?"

"IT IS A PITY SINCE BOTH THE SON AND THE FATHER ARE MISSING OUT ON THE LOVE THEY COULD SHARE."

It's now two a.m. Don's made headway on the two inch thick study binder for General Contractor Licensing. Donny's asleep in his crib in the bedroom and has been since ten o'clock.

Don can hear him stirring but wants to finish the chapter and hopes Penny will take care of him.

As the crying gets loud, Don finds Penny in bed with a quilt piled high above her ears. Fumbling to change a diaper on the kitchen table and prop a bottle up with a roll of paper towels to reach Donny's mouth, he yells for Penny but gets no answer.

An hour later, with Donny asleep, Don is exhausted and downs a couple of beers to relax before falling into bed beside Penny.

With only three hours sleep, Don arrives at work and is groggy. "Don, watch out!" One more step and you'll fall into that hole. You look like you're sleepwalking."

"You're not wrong. I'm having a tough time at home. The baby crying all the time is just too much. I need to study to pass the exam but I can't keep my eyes open."

"Come on in my trailer. I think I can help you. It's nothing bad, just something to give you energy. You'll have no trouble staying awake. Just take one of them each morning."

"I could have told you how this would go. He does not have the strength of character to carry this load on his shoulders and she is not mature enough to bear the daily repetitive chores of motherhood.

"Perhaps they both need to undergo a test of courage and perseverance."

'PERHAPS, AND PERHAPS YOU NEED A BIT MORE PATIENCE."

Six weeks pass and things are looking up for Don and Penny. Little Donny is sleeping through the night which has given Penny the rest she needed and although Don has stayed awake well into the night to study, he feels good about the results.

Sam Jones, Don's Project Manager, greets him one morning.

"Congratulations on passing the Contractor exam so quickly, Don. "I'm being given a promotion to Assistant Vice President. It comes with a new project to manage and I'd like to take you with me.

"We're putting up a 1500 room hotel and need workers we can count on.

"It's a two year job and will mean moving upstate to Ithaca, but you'll have a secure future in the company and it means better pay and more benefits."

Penny was excited at the prospect of moving out of the city, especially since it meant leaving the basement apartment.

Each day since the wedding she had felt the guilty judgment in her mother in law's eyes for her ruining Don's future, although it was never put into words.

They rented a small house with a large yard in Ithaca. Penny pictured a swing set in the yard and hoped to fill the house with more children.

She was delighted with the normal size appliances and found a thrift store with used furniture for the bedrooms and living room.

Arranging a white crocheted doily designed with pineapples on an end table, she placed their prom picture in its silver frame on it. She was still disappointed that her father had decided not to go to the expense of a photographer at the wedding.

Ithaca seemed like a good place for them. She was happy for Don's success at work but was sorry they would be four hours away from her mother.

She called her often to ask questions about caring for Donny as he started to crawl. Today she confided some concerns.

"Don's been working late a lot and often finds excuses to travel to Astoria to spend more time with his high school friend Tom.

"He's so quiet when he gets home and is irritated with Donny's poor attempts at walking."

"Does he come home drunk and hit you?"

"No, I never said that, but he does drink a lot."

"You have no business to complain.

"You reap what you sow, as your father would say if he were here."

"I bet that's from the bible."

"THAT'S RIGHT. GALATIANS 6:7."

Penny didn't say anything more about it, even though it was three a.m. when Don came home that night and left one hundred dollars less than usual on the table for groceries.

The next morning she reminded Don that his mother was coming to help celebrate Donny's first birthday.

She hoped he would come home on time. However, she was not surprised when he did not.

"Let's cut the cake. Daddy probably got stuck at work again. He can have a piece later."

The ringing phone is picked up quickly by little Donny, hoping to hear his Dad's voice. He starts to cry and Penny takes the phone expecting an excuse from Don but is surprised hearing that he's in the hospital.

Don's had an accident at the job site. She regrets the thoughts she'd been having. "I know he's been stressed and I have been pushing him hard."

She left Donny with her mother-in-law and rushed to the hospital.

Don had fallen and injured his back. The emergency room doctor gave him a heavy dose of pain medication and a prescription to take home. He was told to take two weeks off work and to follow up with the family doctor.

Penny was elated. He had escaped a bad injury and would be home for two weeks. That sounded like a vacation to her and a chance to spend time as a family.

She helped him to the car and stopped at the all-night Walgreen's to fill his prescription. Penny looked forward to Don being home. She thought it would mean a better mood and more engagement with Donny and with her.

Two weeks became two months as Don constantly complained about the pain and prescriptions were refilled. The happy family time she hoped for did not happen.

The small amount of money from Workmen's Compensation did not cover their bills and his employer was questioning the status and extent of his back injury.

Don decided to accept the twenty thousand dollars offered by the company to close his claim. His eyes lit up as he was handed the check and he made it clear to Penny that he did not intend to go back to work in construction.

"I'm tired of busting my butt. I'll find a desk job somewhere and this will tide us over."

Penny was not able to keep to her budget or know if Don was paying the rent and other household bills.

Don would stay away days at a time and was belligerent when he got home, complaining of her nagging him when she asked questions.

Realizing that he was no longer merely taking medication for the pain in his back but was addicted to the drugs, Penny was disappointed.

She had sympathized with his pain and ignored his actions but could no longer count on him.

She took a job at the elementary school that Donny would enter in later years and enrolled him in a daycare center nearby.

Although worried that Don might be upset about her not consulting him, she thought it would ease the money situation.

His reaction when she told him chilled her.

"That's good because the money's all gone. You do whatever you want but I'm leaving. I'm tired of working hard to take care of you."

He slammed the door as he left.

Don's friend Tom from Astoria called Penny ten days later.

"Can you come and pick Don up? He's a mess and I have to go to work. He showed up here last night and it looks like he's been sleeping on the street or in some crack house."

Penny felt no sympathy for her husband. "I can't leave work and I'm not sure I want to. You know his parents' house, take him there."

Don's mother answered the door and was shocked at the sight of her son.

His clothes were filthy and his eyes were bloodshot. She was glad his father was not home and rushed to clean Don up and put him to bed. She called Penny's cell phone.

Penny looked at the number calling and declined the call. She figured Don was there by now and she didn't want to talk to him or about him anymore.

With his clothes washed and after a shower and a quick shave of the stubble covering his face, Don was presentable when he sat down at the dinner table. His father was quiet while Don and his mother explained how Penny had treated him so badly, asking him to leave their house.

"It's unfair that our Donny had to get married so young. He didn't get a chance to go to college and now he has to work so hard."

"Okay. You can stay here until you straighten things out with your wife. She'll cool off.

"Meantime, you can go to work with me. You may have to start off as a laborer but it's all I can do right now."

Don slowly finished his meal, borrowed fifty dollars from his mother and said he'd be back in a bit, although he was sure he would not.

'SOMETIMES IT IS DIFFICULT FOR A MOTHER TO SEE FAULT IN HER CHILD AND FINDS IT EASIER TO BLAME SOMEONE ELSE."

"You may be right about his mother, but I told you that marriage was not going to last very long."

PAINFUL HISTORY

Blythe was grateful for Ginger's generosity but finds it hard to rest. Finally falling asleep, her dream begins in a cabin in a Cherokee Nation farming area that also has many white settlers.

"Please add another log to the fire, Father. It's warm enough and the walls of our cabin do hold the heat well but I want to see to keep trying to figure out your new written words. Our Cherokee language is all I've ever known.

"When I hear the white girls talking I understand their language pretty well, but they can carry their words around on leaves of paper and that is a puzzle to me."

"Have patience, Ayoka. Our language has been carried down for generations by word of mouth. It has taken me quite a few years to match sounds to symbols that can be written down and understood.

Several of the men have already become familiar with what I have shown them and you will too."

Bending over to choose a log from the small stack by the side of the stone hearth, he pauses at the sound of a fist striking wood.

"Who could be at our door at this late hour?"

The knock gets louder and Ayoka opens the unlocked door. The Town Chief of the Cherokee community and two other leaders come in.

"Speaking in a formal tone, the Chief states: "Sequoyah, you are charged with witchcraft. It is our belief that with the help of the devil you are able to take the words of our people into your ears and capture them on paper.

"It is my feeling that you should be executed at once to prevent the spread of your black magic any further. However, the new law we enacted recently gives you the right of a civil trial first. We will convene in three days. Be prepared for the consequences of your actions."

Zeus is not pleased with God and his obvious interference with Blythe's sleep after her ordeal.

"What manner of brutality have you had this poor young girl dream of? Has she not suffered enough? Why this frightening dream?

"YOU MISJUDGE MY EFFORTS, BUT YOU WILL SEE. HER DREAM IS ABOUT THE YEAR 1821. IT'S PART OF HER PAST, ONE TO LEARN FROM, NOT TO FEAR."

The stirring of the Gods seems to have the same effect on the young Native American. She tosses in her sleep, fearful that her father will die.

She is twelve year old Ayoka, the daughter of Sequoya, and yet she is Blythe.

Blythe wakes the next day as the sun is setting. Sitting up is painful. Standing is even more painful as she makes her way to the table and sips coffee Ginger has left for her.

There is a note beside the coffee cup. "Think it over." It includes Big Mike's phone number.

She runs to the sink to throw up. She's not sure if it was the thought of last night or the smells permeating the building from the Indian restaurant downstairs.

She recalls her confusing dream.

"Who am I? Was Sequoyah my ancestor and was my dream some kind of message. I know my mother is Cherokee but she never mentioned him or the girl Ayoka."

There's a computer on a table. "Maybe I can get a signal from downstairs."

She successfully looks up "Sequoyah" on the internet.

"Sequoyah was a silversmith and a leader of the Cherokee community which had integrated many white settlers. He was born around 1765 in an area that is now Knoxville, Tennessee.

"He was raised by his mother, who belonged to the Red Paint Clan of the Cherokee Nation. His father was half Cherokee and his paternal grandfather was a white trader.

“He was intrigued with the ability of the written words of the white people. The only language his people knew was Cherokee spoken verbally.

“There were thousands of sounds that the people used in making themselves understood. It took Sequoya more than ten years to develop eighty-five symbols that could serve as the basis for the Cherokee written language.”

“Well, if that’s some kind of message from my Cherokee ancestors it definitely says don’t go home.

“My father must be in bad shape since I didn’t come home last night and I don’t want to add to my mom’s problems.”

It’s a year later and the motel where Ginger recommended Blythe for a job has been shut down by the police for a month now. They were tired of raiding and arresting the prostitutes who would be freed in hours.

Cleaning bathrooms each morning had given Blythe money for food and a bed for a few hours before the girls brought customers in at night.

It’s been an hour since the police car stopped and Blythe had to move her large cardboard box. She found a dark corner a few blocks away from there and set it up again.

The trash cans behind the big hotel were empty tonight and her stomach is growling. She’s tired and hungry as she raises a sheet of newspaper over her head.

But God is not quite finished with the lesson and is prepared when she falls asleep.

The same dream continues with Sequoyah now looking more like Blythe's father explaining how he developed the translation of the Cherokee written language into usable written English words.

"In that way our knowledge can be printed in books and our documents can be saved for future generations."

The Chief is not convinced. "I do not believe that is possible. We must conclude that you are guilty of devilish ways."

Blythe feels cold although the fire burns brightly. One of the warriors that had already benefited from the knowledge of reading that Sequoya has taught him quickly suggests a test. "Let Ayoka show you."

It is agreed and Ayoka is led outside where two women guard her and assure the Chief that she could not possibly see or hear her father from that distance.

Blythe is now very aware of her surroundings. Although it is dark, she sees that the cabin is in the midst of a small town with one short dirt road and a few shuttered shops.

Inside Sequoyah is told to write a message on a small piece of paper using the symbols he has devised for the language of the Cherokees.

He tells the group of men what he has written.
"Do not be afraid, child, these are our brothers."

The women lead Ayoka back and watch carefully as she takes the slip of paper.

Ayoka has barely mastered the language of the written words and she accepts the paper nervously.

Blythe feels the dream moccasins on her feet and the fringe of the native dress at her wrists. Terror grips her as she realizes the importance of her task.

She remembers the many times her own father has told her to have no fear and be courageous.

Ayoka reads the words on the paper aloud in Cherokee. There is a murmur of disbelief.

The women take her aside once more.

She then writes back, "I am not afraid, father," using the new letters and indicating her understanding. One of the women hurries to the Chief with the note.

After several messages where it was clear that the Cherokee words were being used correctly, Blythe no longer fears the outcome of the trial.

A large book now appears then in her dream. The page is open to "Cherokee Council Meetings in the Year 1829."

Blythe can read it clearly even though it is not written in English.

Tuesday, October 20 – "Bill is passed providing for publication, in pamphlet form, a series of essays on "the present crisis of the American Indians."

Blythe is caught up in the dream. She wonders what went wrong.

"What crisis?" She continues reading.

Saturday, October 24—"On motion of Choonnagkee of Chickamauga District, an old law making death the penalty for selling any lands in treaty without the authority of the nation was committed to writing and up for adoption."

"An eighty year old man rises to speak. "My children. Permit me to call you so, as I am an old man and have lived a long time.

"I have watched the well being of this Nation.

"I love your lives and wish our people to increase on the land of our fathers. There are wicked men who may arise to cede away our country contrary to our consent.

"My sun of existence is fast approaching to its setting and my aged bones will soon be laid under ground, and I wish them buried in the bosom of this earth we have received from our fathers who had it from the Great Being above.

"My feeble limbs will not allow me to stand longer. I can say no more, but before I sit allow me to tell you that I am in favor of the bill."

Blythe sees the old man clearly and is reading the words before her eyes in black and white but she remembers in vivid color her own grandfather at eihty years old and feels a personal sadness for this old man.

"Andrew Jackson was elected President of the United States in November 1828. In his first Annual Message to Congress, President Jackson stated:

"The consequences of a speedy removal will be important to the United States, to the individual States, and to the Indians themselves.

"It puts an end to all possible danger of collision between the authorities of the General and State Governments on account of the Indians. It will place a dense and civilized population in large tracts of country now occupied by a few savage hunters."

In 1829, Sequoyah and 2,500 Cherokees were moved by the U.S. government to the "Indian Territory" which is now Oklahoma. The land there was exchanged for the land they had been living on for generations.

President Jackson signed the Indian Removal Act on May 28, 1830.

"This tale indicates that many of these people must have suffered.

"IT WAS A DAY OF GREAT SADNESS."

Blythe wakes and for the first time shed tears for herself and what happened to her, tears for her father, tears for her mother and tears for all Native Americans.

"I'm not ready to go home, but it is a new beginning."

Blythe picks up the stack of newspapers that have sheltered her and looks for the Help Wanted pages. She nudges an old woman sleeping beside a rusted supermarket cart overflowing with plastic bags filled with her belongings.

"Come on, Sadie. We can do better than this. I hear there's a shelter over on thirty-second."

THE BLACK KNIGHT

Maurice is sitting in the sand with his rifle by his side. Three other soldiers are resting against the same building trying to stay in the shade. Two small barefooted boys are sitting quietly close by in the sun, but their eyes and ears aren't missing anything.

"Pack up your gear guys. Trucks are ready to get us out of here. It looks like we'll be surrounded by the Syrian army shortly. We only have a small window and have to clear out.

"The SDF can't hold out any longer even with our help. The bombing's been relentless and won't be getting any better."

"I know," Maurice tells the soldier sitting next to him.

"It hasn't stopped since I got here four months ago."

Maurice scoops up a bit of sand in his hand and lets it drip slowly through his fingers as he remembers when he first arrived. The others lean over to listen as he begins talking.

"They told me I was going to teach," he said slowly.

"I kept hoping for the mechanic's pool because I'm pretty good around an engine, but the closest I got to working on a car was to help haul the bombed wrecks out of the path of our trucks.

"My bull's eye record on the target was so good that they decided that I should teach people how to shoot in this godforsaken place.

"The first time I tried, the blank look on the faces of my students told me I was failing.

"The worst part was trying to prepare them for what they were in for and how to react. They were being asked to face certain death at a very young age.

"I found a dust covered baseball bat and put it in the hands of the youngest looking Kurd.

"Then I asked the translator to tell him to imagine a baseball coming right at him. The young kid set his legs apart and swung the bat hard with a knowing look and smiled.

"Everyone clapped and laughed. It might have been a bat they were familiar playing with.

"Now," I told the translator, "tell him to close his eyes and imagine the ball turning into bullets from an AK47 and to realize that it's been pitched by his cousin hidden behind a turned over car."

"There was a bewildered look on the kid's face as the translator finished translating what I said.

"QUICKLY, I shouted at him, SHOOT MAN, SHOOT, and he dropped the bat in panic.

"No one laughed. I think they got it. At least they practiced more and fooled around less.

"This young man definitely has the blood of a knight running in his veins."

"YOU ARE MAKING PROGRESS,.ZEUS YOU PRAISE HIM ALTHOUGH HE REPRESENTS CHRISTIANITY."

"You misunderstand. This brave man helping others to learn does not represent any given religion, but the goodness in mankind, I am surprised you do not see that."

"I DO UNDERSTAND AND SEE THAT YOU HAVE LEARNED A VERY IMPORTANT LESSON."

"After that the translator, whose name was Joe, or something that sounded close enough to it, hung out with me whenever I took a break.

"He smoked some nasty smelling cigarettes and I chewed some Juicy Fruit gum he didn't like the smell of, but we worked it out.

"What did you have to talk about with the Kurdish guy? Did you talk about this crazy war?" One of the men gathered around Maurice asked as they kept listening, glad to have something to distract them.

Joe, the translator, had been sent here along with Maurice and the other men and was sitting nearby. He smiled at the soldier's questions and Maurice's answer.

"There was no talk about the fighting. Joe had been a history teacher until a year ago when he was recruited because he spoke English and French and of course his native Kurdish. He told me that at one time this part of the world was known as the cradle of civilization.

"He would go on with details of how the alphabet, music, art, engineering and trade had their roots in the desert and he thought our modern culture would benefit by more education of his world.

"History is very interesting," he said one night. "It has a way of repeating itself.

"Right down the road a few kilometers is the town of Afrin, the same town that Homer described as the place where the thousand ships gathered to wage war against Troy."

"I politely feigned interest. Homer was a funny guy on a comic television show but I didn't remember any skit about a thousand ships.

"We had agreed to listen without questioning and Joe honored that agreement by listening to me for hours about how I would own a garage one day and it would specialize in classic cars like Jaguars.

"I skipped the part of how the Jaguar helped get me here."

The sergeant broke into Maurice's thoughts.

"How about it? When the trucks get here be ready to load up quickly."

Joe watched as they waited. He was scheduled to remain and approached the group along with the two boys as the trucks arrived.

Another thought suddenly hit Maurice.

"What should we do about the kids?

Maurice looks over at Houman, the ten year old Muslim boy he's been sharing his food with for weeks. When he first started following him around Maurice was reminded of himself at that age.

He would have fit in easily with the boys back home on his street since he looked very much like they did.

Maurice spoke up again.

"What do we do about the kids, Sarge?"

"Our orders are to move on."

"But they'll try to hide when they hear the planes coming and there are no school buildings left standing and their homes are a target."

"The UN's working out a plan for a safe conduct convoy to get them out. Our orders are to evacuate *now*, so get a move on."

Houman understood enough to figure out what was happening but he sat quietly fingering a candy wrapper.

"You'll be okay, kid. There'll be trucks coming for you soon too, but I have to go now."

The boy sat still, his dry eyes open wide. There was nothing that could surprise him now or make him cry any more.

"Xwede bi me re be" were the only words he spoke.

"God be with us" translated Joe as he took the boy's hand and they walked slowly away.

Maurice watched them go past the ruins of houses on both sides of the street. He took a last look and closed his eyes to shut out the horror of Aleppo. The once thriving city Joe had described was reduced to rubble.

Maurice hadn't seen it any other way.

He knew this part of Syria and the people who lived here had been fighting for many years. He'd been told how important it was for his Special Forces Unit to guide and train the SDF fighters.

He had to admire the people facing such terror each day but was totally confused about who was right and what they were fighting about.

"If peace ever comes," he thought, "it would have been built on dead bodies and piled up stones."

Maurice jumped in the waiting truck and found a place quickly, eager to get away from the memory of the boy's dark eyes.

Willing himself to sleep to clear his mind of his role in the drama surrounding him, he shuts his eyes tight.

Maurice keeps hearing Houman's blessing "God be with us, God be with us" over and over until he falls asleep, slumped over in his seat.

He can see Houman's face in his dream. His dark eyes are bright and his mouth is moving but the strange words Maurice hears are in a deep mature voice and what he said was odd.

"He was all black, even as I tell ye: His body
and his hands were all black, saving only his

teeth. His shield and his armor were even
those of a Moor, and black as a raven…

Had they not heard him call upon God no man had dared face him, deeming that he was the devil or one of his fellows out of hell, for that his steed was so great, and he was taller even than Sir Lancelot.

"Saga of Morien" – Knight of the Crusade

"WHY HAVE YOU INTRODUCED THE CRUSADES?

"ONCE MORE YOU TRY MY PATIENCE."

Zeus doesn't mind the rebuke.

"Your Son and the Pope had a field day with the knights falling over themselves to fight for their honor. Our student needs to dig deep, a bit further back."

Maurice now finds himself astride a huge black horse. "Whoa. I've never ridden a horse before. It feels like I'm ten feet off the ground and my power matches that of this animal. The horse's breath clouds the air but I don't feel the cold. This metal vest is so heavy. I know I'm dreaming but this city seems familiar.

"The tower high on that hill looks like the ones in Aleppo where the Muslims used to go to pray every day, but it's much bigger and has more intricate detail."

He notices a knight on foot holding a boy that looks like Houman. The boy's mother is lying on the ground screaming.

"ZEUS, THE CRUSADES HAPPENED. IT'S PART OF THE HISTORY OF THE CHURCH. NO NEED TO DWELL ON IT."

"Looks like Maurice will be there in time to see another part of history. Let's shine a little light on the times and make sure he sees it in the eyes of a black knight."

Maurice turns to the knight riding next to him. "That lightening strike was blinding."

"There was no lightening. Your eyes deceive you and your mind wanders. After six days in battle, my very bones ache and my mind has left me, as has yours."

"That was no battle for you. You chased the women down for your own pleasure and enjoyed using your short blade on their sons. The young girls you took will make decent slaves. No, the victory in battle was mine. I fought with honor and the people of Aleppo will not see another sunrise.

"I will be rewarded in heaven for the Muslim blood that I spilled."

"Stop, stop!!" Maurice yells, shocked awake by the horror of his own thoughts.

"Stop what buddy? I'm just sittin' here."

The men become silent and the only sound until they reach their destination hours later is the hum of the truck's engine.

Maurice is now at his next post and no longer thinks about Houman or Aleppo or anything but staying alive.

There are so many Muslim boys hounding his patrol, asking questions and begging for sweets.

There is a moment of silence to be sure the raid is over and no more missiles are falling from the sky. Then he hears the children crying, sees the children bleeding, and knows many children are dying. They have severe burns, missing limbs and blackened clothing. Maurice thinks he can smell gas fumes coming off each one of them.

Actually, he doesn't seem to think at all anymore. He eats, sleeps, cleans his weapon and shakes insects out of his boots.

He was only supposed to train, he wasn't supposed to fire except when fired upon. "A matter of life or death," the sergeant said, "either yours or his."

No, Maurice didn't want to fire, but Maurice didn't want to die. He didn't want to see the skinny young soldier fall. He didn't want to watch him bleed and didn't want to look into his eyes.

He never meant to notice that his skin was dark, much like his own. He didn't want to hear his outcry.

He knew enough of the language and forced himself to listen to the fallen soldier's plea.

"Please take my Quran. Keep it near your heart and absorb it through your uniform."

He didn't throw up until he was out of sight of the quiet body. What started as shock became terrible guilt and an intense desire to atone for his perceived misdeed, even though it was his duty.

The frayed copy of the Quran that the fatally wounded soldier gave him is in his pocket.

He asked the Kurdish interpreter what the book really was.

"It's like a guide for mankind," he had replied. Maurice gave him his Foster Grant sunglasses in trade for teaching the verses to him.

Each day now when he hears the piercing call, he picks up his prayer rug and hurries to the shell of a building that was once a finely decorated mosque. He's not alone in the mosque.

A few dozen Muslim men lean down in prayer with him. He is searching for hope and forgiveness. As the Muezzin calls the prayers, Maurice recites along using the words taught him.

"God! There is no deity but Him, the Alive, the Eternal. Neither slumber nor sleep overtaketh Him. Unto Him belongeth whatsoever is in the heavens and whatsoever is in the earth. Who is he that intercedeth with Him save by His leave. He knoweth that which is in front of them and that which is behind them, while they encompass nothing of His knowledge save what He wills. His throne includeth the heavens and the earth," and He is never weary of preserving them. He is the Sublime, the Tremendous."

Surah Al-Baqarah 2.255.

During the prayers, Maurice's mind often travels back to the few times when he attended a church service with his mother. Except for the songs being sung louder and the congregation showing more enthusiasm at home, the words in the mosque seemed much the same.

"He has a point there. The Muezzin even sounds like a psalti with the high pitched voice who sings out the prayers in the Greek Orthodox Church."

Most of the men in his unit ignore Maurice going to the mosque, but some are quite upset with what they call fraternizing, even though the Muslims attending services with Maurice are their allies.

They're relieved when he receives orders returning him to the States and chalk up Maurice's behavior to trauma.

It's been two years since the Judge offered Maurice what he thought was a very easy choice. He was urged to re-enlist, and simply shook his head in reply.

He questions his choice in court.

"No, I did the right thing. But now it's time to go home."

PERSEPHONE

QUEEN OF THE PROM

"Young Ellen brings Persephone to my mind. She was the Goddess of Spring, my own daughter born to Demeter, Goddess of the Earth. She was the pride and joy of her mother and was watched over carefully.

"All was well until one day Persephone's beauty attracted my brother Hades, who abducted her.

"Her captivity led to the dark period of grief that Demeter went through, unable to detect what had happened to her beloved daughter. Since she was Goddess of the Earth, her suffering was shared by all mortals. The darkness descended and the grasses withered and all the crops died.

"It's a long journey of Demeter seeking her daughter, a story of love, separation, grief, and finally celebration when it was agreed that Persephone would be shared. The light would be restored for the Spring, when the seeds spurt forth and Persephone would then dwell with her mother on Earth.

"Of course Hades was paid his due and the darkness of Winter returned to the Earth when Persephone returned to the underworld each year to her place as Hades wife.

"Her story is one of abduction. It is a story of light and of darkness, of Winter and of Spring."

"A TALE OF FAMILY FRICTION AS MODERN TODAY AS IT WAS IN YOUR TIME. BUT OFTEN THE STORY DOES NOT END SO WELL.

"NOW WE HAVE ELLEN. ONLY ONE YEAR AGO, SHE WAS A VISION IN WHITE WALKING DOWN THE CHURCH AISLE WITH HER LONG BLONDE TRESSES SHINING AND HER SHEER VEIL TRAILING GRACEFULLY BEHIND HER. SHE WAS ADMIRED BY ALL.

"SHE STILL THOUGHT OF HERSELF AS A BEAUTY QUEEN JUST AS IT HAD BEEN ORDAINED ON THE NIGHT OF THEIR HIGH SCHOOL PROM. HENRY HAD A CHOICE OF OFFERS TO PLAY FOOTBALL.

"HE WAS CONSIDERED A FUTURE STAR AND DREW ATTENTION FROM THE MEDIA.

THERE WAS A VERY LARGE BONUS INVOLVED IN HIS SIGNING SO THEY HAD NO FINANCIAL WORRIES."

"Ellen has spent her days shopping, adding to her already ample supply of clothing and cosmetics. Her beauty is intact.

"See how she checks the mirror image often, but her own reflection is not enough. Her beauty had always been admired by others.

"Now here she is in black shirt and tight black jeans riding on the back of a motorcycle driven by a man that is not her husband Henry. She has dyed the blonde tresses of her wedding day black and her long hair flows loosely behind her.

"She may be related to Persephone, but this is no abduction. It is obvious she goes willingly."

"IT IS APPARENT THAT HERCULES IS UNAWARE OF HER ACTIONS.

"HE IS AN HONORABLE MAN ALWAYS DETERMINED TO DO HIS BEST. HE STRIVES TO MEET EACH CHALLENGE IN THE GAME WITH STRENGTH AND DETERMINATION.

"You forget the frailties of my gods. Hercules had no thoughts of others as he garnered the prize.

"What of Ellen? True, she has the jewels and enjoys the spoils, but the dark days take her. She now competes for his attention and misses the admiration of other men."

"HENRY SIGNED A CONTRACT AND MUST TRAVEL. HE IS TRUE TO HIS WORD AND LOYAL TO HIS TEAMMATES."

"She grieves for a time when her beauty was enough to sustain her. She is deprived of the adulation she thinks is her due. Her husband receives all the attention now.

"Magazine covers with his handsome face and 'Go Hercules' on the sports pages do not help and blot out the good days in her mind."

"YOU SEEM TO DEFEND HER WILES."

"Persephone's stay with my brother in the Underworld gave everyone on Earth a taste of the cold darkness that she left on Earth.

"Ellen lives those dark days and is willing to seek the pleasures that brighten them, even though the light of her beauty is fleeting and will not last. I do not defend, but I do understand."

"THOSE ARE YOUR MYTHS. THE SEASONS ON EARTH ARE NATURAL HAPPENINGS AND THERE IS NO REASON TO CONNECT WINTER WITH YOUR BROTHER."

"Ellen has run the gamut of Persephone's emotions. Everyone on Earth rejoiced at the return of Spring. Perhaps Ellen will have reason to celebrate Hercules' return. We shall see."

GOD MEETS ZEUS

There are two motorcycles parked in the driveway as the crowded minivan pulls up at Ellen and Henry's house.

Last night the coach decided that they would push on to reach home instead of stopping at the pre-arranged motel.

"Whoa, Herc. Who's been keeping your wife company at your house while you go make the bread."

"You guys are nuts. Ellen and I have been together since grade school and she's true to me. There's something wrong here. We don't know any bikers."

The teasing stops and one of the team members brings in a somber thought.

"Everybody knows our schedule and when you'll be away. Maybe they broke in."

"Oh my God. Ellen…" Henry starts for the door, fearing the worst. Two of his friends grab him before he gets there.

"If we're right, then you better be careful. They may have forced their way in knowing you were out of town and they could be armed. Some of those bikers belong to gangs.

"We better go in with you. I'm taking the tire iron. You got your knife, Johnny?"

"Here, Henry, take my knife. I always carry it for protection."

Henry quietly unlocks the door and swings it open into the living room.

Ellen screams and removes herself from the lap of one of the men. She reaches for her robe on the back of the sofa.

Confused, his anger rising rapidly, Henry lunges at Ellen's companion who stood up to defend himself.

The second biker quickly jumps on Henry's back and Henry's teammates join in to stop the foe much as they have in every football game, forming a jumbled mass of bodies on the floor of the living room.

The struggle is over quickly. It's difficult to say how it happened but there is a lot of blood and Johnny's knife is protruding from Hercules' lifeless body.

"She is not Persephone's descendant after all, but may well be the child of Helen, the one whose beautiful face sank one thousand ships and caused the death of those she loved and the destruction of the city of Troy.

GOD'S DILEMNA

Looking for some signs of hope, God reviews the actions of the twelve young people chosen to help guide his decision on the future of the universe.

"MY FEARS HAVE NOT YET ABATED. THE FUTURE LOOKS BLEAK.

"You often remind me to be patient. More time is needed to change the course of the world."

"YOU ARE RIGHT WHEN YOU SPEAK OF MY IMPATIENCE, HOWEVER I SEE THE WORLD DETERIORATING DAILY. I MUST CONSIDER IF THE MORTALS ARE ON THE RIGHT PATH."

"You must give credit where it's due. The young black warrior served out the penalty for his short joy ride. He will not steal again."

"TRUE, BUT THE DEMONS OF DOUBT DISTURB HIS REST.

"HE'S TROUBLED AND CONFUSED ABOUT MAN'S CHOICE OF ENEMIES AND HIS OWN PART IN THE HISTORY OF WAR.

"AND DON IS STILL ON HIS JOURNEY IN ODYSSEUS WAKE."

"I admit .that I have very little hope for Don. He reminds me of many fallen gods. Old habits are hard to break.

"However, Blythe, the girl who was betrayed and lost her innocence would have made my goddesses proud to call her sister. She suffered and yet found the inner strength to recover and kindness of heart to help others."

"Speaking of demons, you should be aware that Hades vowed to corrupt the morals of our chosen dozen. Perhaps he was instrumental in the evils that beset them."

"I AM A BIT SURPRISED THAT YOU DO NOT REALIZE THAT THE DEVIL BY ANY NAME IS NOT ABLE TO ACCOMPLISH EVIL WITHOUT THE COOPERATION OF MORTALS."

Zeus is unwilling to concede that his brother has no power since it would cloud the belief of his own existence. It is better to change the subject.

"I do see a ray of light shining on our Mexican child. She is formidable in her imaginings and has proven more so in reality. Her friend Max is supportive although he too seeks answers."

"BUT IS HER QUEST ATTAINABLE OR MORE LIKE THE IDYLLIC WANDERINGS OF DON QUIXOTE?

"That reference eludes me."

"I DO MOURN THE UNTIMELY DEATH OF OUR HERCULES.

"His star did shine brightly, but for so short a time. Henry did win many awards and signified the strength and endurance of man and was a reminder of the athletes of Olympia."

"HE HAD A BEAUTIFUL BRIDE BUT GOT LOST IN HERO WORSHIP AND AVOIDED HIS WIFE'S PROBLEMS. YOUR COMPARISON TO THE SEIGE OF TROY IS ACCURATE - VANITY DID PLAY A PART."

"I think we must consider those two as failures, although Ellen bears a large part of their misfortune.

"It is regrettable that Jesus did not include women among his disciples. It might have sent a message that would change centuries of dissension.

"Women can be most useful in maintaining the peace and sometimes in starting a war. They have the spine of a tiger that won't back down, the wings of a dove in beautiful flight, and the bite of a shark. Their weapons are at hand but only drawn when they are provoked."

"YOU SOUND LIKE A MORTAL WITH MUCH EXPERIENCE AT THE HANDS OF WHAT IS REFERRED TO AS A WEAKER SEX."

"Do I sense a smile and ridicule of my accurate description of women?"

"LET US CONCLUDE OUR SUMMARY OF THE VALUE OF OUR SELECTED GROUP.

"OUR OTHER FOUR MAKE MERRY IN TEXAS IN WAYS TYPICAL OF THE YOUTH OF TODAY. THIS DOES NOT PORTEND ANY COURAGEOUS ACTS ON BEHALF OF EARTH."

"He does not admit how pleased he is with Michael, his mortal spirit. Zeus continues to be pleased by any action of Athena and attempts to defend her.

"Not so. The girl Athena studies to achieve the knowledge to help the sick and often volunteers to aid in the efforts to feed the homeless.

"Much to her credit she clings to her virginity."

"BUT HAVE THEY SHOWN ME ENOUGH? MORTALS OFTEN SAY WHAT FOOLS THEY WERE WHEN THEY REGRET THEIR ACTIONS, AS IF THE JESTER CAME AND BLINDFOLDED THEM.

"I FEEL THE FOOL MYSELF. I AM THE CREATOR. I NEVER SOUGHT POWER OVER MORTALS. I GAVE UP CONTROL BY PLACING HUMAN BEINGS ABOVE ALL THE CREATURES ON EARTH WITH AN INTELLECT TO LEAD,

"I THOUGHT THEY UNDERSTOOD THAT THEY WOULD BE THE CARETAKERS OF THE EARTH.

"MY DISAPPOINTMENT SHOWS THAT IT WAS WISHFUL THINKING."

"This is not the first time you have been so disappointed.

"Do you not remember the very words in the first book of the bible?

"And it repented the Lord that he had made man on the Earth, and that every imagination of the thoughts of his heart was only evil continuously. Genesis 6:5

"I will destroy man whom I have created from the face of the earth." Genesis 6:7

"Supposedly one time an old man named Noah talked you out of it by building the Ark.

"Remember, length 300 cubits; breadth 50 cubits, height 30, window, three stories – or maybe he just used his mortal initiative and built a big boat so as not to drown in the flood.

"Perhaps the man was simply smart enough to predict the rain would come and it had no relation to your anger. Others may have injected their own thoughts into your words and they have been misinterpreted.

"Why now has mankind become such a burden to you? Why the desire to punish them for not doing the right thing when the definition of 'free will' has no such distinction?

"Or is your vanity at stake here? Perhaps you seek only a world as you perceived it, at peace with man in harmony with nature."

"YOU OVERSTEP ONCE MORE, ZEUS. BUT YOU DO NOT HEAR THEIR ANGUISH AND PLEAS FOR MERCY. THEY DO NOT ASK *YOU* WHY YOU ALLOW SUCH EVIL DOING AND HUMAN SUFFERING."

DON'S ODYSSEY

The sound of an ambulance siren is ominous, most especially at night when you are eagerly awaiting it.

Tom is relieved to hear it in the distance as the siren grows louder and stops in front of his apartment building where he's been pacing impatiently.

"Hurry, hurry. I can't wake him up."

Two paramedics unload a stretcher and follow Tom inside. Don is lying on the floor.

"I found him slumped against my door when I came home and I dragged him inside."

The paramedics ask questions as they work on Don.

"Yes, I know him. We went to the same high school."

Don mumbled when asked his name, but it was not understood.

"No, I have no idea what he took. I wasn't even home."

"I tire of watching this chosen mortal fall.

"He may be a cousin to Dionysius whose vice of choice was wine but he was a jolly drunk, not morose as this one."

"PATIENCE IS CERTAINLY NOT ONE OF YOUR VIRTUES, ZEUS, NOR IS FAITH IN THE BONDS OF MARRIAGE.

"HOWEVER IT IS ALSO MY THOUGHT TO CHALLENGE THIS YOUNG MAN AS YOU SUGGEST. HE MUST OVERCOME THE OBSTACLES AND CAST OFF THE DESIRE TO IMBIBE AND STRAY FROM HOME.

"PENELOPE STAYS THE COURSE OF MARRIAGE AND YOUNG LOVE BUT SHE MAY SOON TIRE OF BEING THE PATIENT WIFE."

"Penelope the patient wife. Now there's a name that rings a bell in the halls of my memory.

"For years her husband Odysseus wandered yet she had open arms for him when he returned home."

"THAT WAS THEN BUT WOMEN DO NOT FEEL BOUND TO ONE MAN TODAY. THEIR VOWS OF LOVE ARE EXPRESSED MORE FREELY."

"That does remind me of my good old days."

"ALL TOO TRUE, BUT THE RESULTING SEXUAL FREEDOM IS NOT LOVE."

"So, animal instinct sometimes prevails over love."

God chooses to ignore Zeus' last remark.

"I REGRET GIVING UP ON DON. HE DOES REPRESENT MANY MORTALS IN THE WORLD WITH ADDICTION PROBLEMS."

"Perhaps he should undergo hardships and wander much as Odysseus did."

"LET IT BE SO.

"A similar journey could set an example of temptation and perseverance overcoming obstacles and test both Don and Penny."

"WE WILL SEE IF HIS MIND AND BODY CAN ABSORB THE LESSON AND SURVIVE. BUT WE WILL NOT INTERFERE WITH HIS FREE WILL.

"HOWEVER MUCH WE INFLUENCE HIS THOUGHTS, HIS ACTIONS WILL BE OF HIS OWN DOING, WHETHER GOOD OR EVIL."

In motions they had performed many times, the paramedics lift Don onto the stretcher and call ahead to the hospital as they prepare to leave.

Don is babbling something about high waves and he doesn't respond to their questions about it.

As the ambulance siren begins, Don holds his head and places his hands tight against his ears.

He knew they should not listen to the siren call of the monster Scylla. "Cover your ears men! Don't listen to her evil trap to get you."

Don sees himself in a boat in the raging sea and a beautiful mermaid suddenly turns into a monster with four eyes and six long legs and she's coming after him.

There were heads of dogs ringed around her waist to devour sailors who listened to her call.

"He believes what he sees is Scylla the beautiful mermaid who lived in the sea and was turned into a monster by Circe the Sorceress."

"HIS DREAM IS NOT UNLIKE MANY HALLUCINATIONS OF THE ADDICTED."

Don now sees the four eyes as Penny's eyes and the long tentacles wrapped around his throat are now her arms and he has trouble breathing.

"Men, please help me with this wheel. I don't know how to steer a boat and the wind is picking up. The waves are getting higher and stronger. I can't hold on much longer. Head for that small island before the boat capsizes."

"Into the Land of the Lotus Eaters, very fitting. Let's see how he handles the Cyclops."

Don finds himself in a dark cave and he believes a one-eyed monster is trying to grab one of his men to eat him. He strikes out at the light on the forehead of the medic trying to get his vital signs as they head for the hospital.

The paramedics decide to strap him in a straightjacket as his whole body is squirming on the stretcher and his arms keep reaching out.

When Tom had called and told her where to find Don, Penny had hesitated.

She thought it was just one more time and he would recover and do the same thing again.

She was tired. She called his parents and was not surprised when his father refused to go to the hospital and hung up.

She knew that his parents had been going through the same ups and downs with Don, but is not comfortable hearing that they have given up too. She decides to check on him at the hospital.

Placing Don on the hospital bed, the paramedics prepare to leave. “He’s all yours, Doc. He’ll probably make it, but his mind’s a bit whacked. I’m guessing heroin, but got no info.

Penny has been standing at the doorway and has heard Don’s mutterings and struggle with reality. He is hardly recognizable as the handsome young man she had fallen in love with.

“It’s so dark in here. I must be in hell. Somebody please help me.”

Don’s words were clear.

The sight of her husband in his delirium had upset her, but his words were what touched her heart.

“If I love him and don’t help him, who will?”

She signs the papers subjecting him to thirty days observation and reflects on how their lives could have gone so wrong.

She knows it will take some time and patience and vows to herself to make changes and help him overcome his addiction.

“It may be best to tell her how Penelope endured for seven years and welcomed her husband back.”

“NO NEED. SHE HAS THE MATTER IN HAND.”

LIGHT IN THE DARKNESS

Maurice welcomes the sun coming through the chintz curtains in the kitchen window as his mother pours him a second cup of coffee.

"I'm so glad you're home safe, son. Was it as bad as the reports on the news. The awful photos of those little kids on stretchers were heartbreaking."

He's been home a few weeks. He hasn't spoken of his time in Syria and does not reply to the question.

"I'm going for a walk, Mom. See who I can find."

Finding Petey wasn't hard. He was on Astoria Boulevard in front of Walgreen's having a smoke. Maurice's mother had mentioned that he worked there.

Their hands reached out and did a turn before ending in a fist slap.

"What's up, Petey?"

"Not much. Your mother brags to my mother about you in church. "Any medals? Were you a hero or something? Looks like you still got your arms and legs."

Maurice ignores the remarks meant to be taken lightly.

"Seen Mike?"

"Not likely. He's back in. Only got one year on the Jag but probation was too hard.

"All that peeing in a cup and being polite to the Man was not for our Mikey. He got three years this time. They sent him to Riker's Island.

"Got to get back in to work. Let me know if you need a job, I'll put in a good word with the manager."

Maurice keeps walking on Astoria Boulevard, not wanting to go home yet. Home's too neat and clean and his mother hovers over him.

A sign catches his eye, "Astoria Islamic Center."

It's a plain red brick building, nothing like a mosque. Maurice had asked his mother about the two women he saw on their street wearing burkas. She told him that there are quite a few Muslims living in the neighborhood and have been for years.

"I never noticed before," he had replied.

Now he walks into the Center and quietly kneels in prayer. He doesn't speak to anyone and avoids eye contact. No one at the Center questions his being there.

"AH, THE RESULTS OF WAR. THERE ARE A GROWING NUMBER OF VETERANS OF WARS IN MANY PLACES AROUND THE WORLD SUFFERING AND UNABLE TO RETRIEVE THE SAME LIFE THEY HAD BEFORE THEY WERE TRAINED TO KILL.

"MANY OF THEM CAN BE FOUND AMONG THE HOMELESS WHO WANDER THE STREETS."

"The commandment not to kill may have been appropriate for the time that the bible was written, but not for today and certainly not for when I was considered ruler of my kingdom. Why even the young boys were trained to fight in Sparta. There were no equals in battle and we are still proud of their bravery. Dying is part of living, and killing is part of man."

"WOULD THAT IT WERE NOT SO."

Maurice goes to the Muslim center quite regularly. He's grown a bushy beard and wears loose fitting dark clothing. Some evenings, on his walk home, he stops at a small park and plays with a basketball often left there.

He puts it through the hoop, retrieves the ball, and shoots again, moving slowly in motion with the ball, over and over again.

If there's a game going, he walks away. After several silent turn-downs from Maurice, the men stop asking him to join in.

It's almost dark tonight and he takes a shot. Bouncing off the rim, the ball goes to the right and is quickly picked up and tossed at the ring. Once through, one bounce brings it to Maurice and without looking over at the other player Maurice sends it up again.

In the dim light of evening, the one-on-one game proceeds with two sweating players and fast action on the court. The only sound is the bounce of the ball and the swish of the net.

Maurice takes a few side glances at the tall slender figure in black tee shirt, tight jeans and dark hair in a long pony tail. Once or twice the face of the woman comes close to his. She seems as tall as he is and her skin looks dark but not like his.

When the street light comes on, he sees that her skin is not black, but light brown with a red tint. They each give up trying hard to win and sit up against the chain link fence. She reaches for a backpack and offers him a drink from her water bottle.

"You're not a black male. How come you play basketball so well?"

"You don't have to be black or male to throw the ball around."

"No, but it helps, and it helps to be six feet tall like you."

"Maurice, I'm only five foot eleven, but I *can* jump pretty high."

"How do you know my name?"

"I guess you never noticed me in high school. My name is Blythe, Blythe Waneek."

Maurice turns and looks at her. "The Indian girl. Yeah, I remember you, but you were never this tall."

Blythe laughs pleasantly. "You're just being kind. I *was* this tall and a whole lot wider. They called me Miss Six by Six and they made sure they captured me eating a big piece of pizza for a yearbook photo.

"I have to confess, Maurice. I saw you at the Muslim Center and followed you.

"I won't ask any questions and you needn't tell me your story. I've been helped through my hard times and now I pass it along wherever I can.

"If you need a place to stay, or just to hang out, there's a center run by some veterans over on thirty-ninth Street off Astoria. There's a court for basketball and they serve meals if you're interested."

"My Mom's a good cook and I have a soft bed to sleep on, but I may stop by some time.

"Thanks for not asking questions. Can I ask just one?

"Shoot."

Maurice's face screws up at the word and he takes a deep breath. Blythe notices and waits quietly.

"How did you make the change? I mean, you're beautiful and you were really heavy and I do remember making fun of you myself. How did you get it together ?"

It was Blythe's turn to take a deep breath before answering.

"It was very hard, Maurice. I'll be able to talk about it some time, but not yet.

"Now I need some courage. My Mom's a good cook too, but I haven't been home since the night of the prom. I just don't know if I'd be welcome. I regret now that I didn't appreciate my parents and their problems. They have every right to disown me."

"C'mon girl. I'll walk you home.

"Xwede bi me re be. God will be with us."

MEMORIES

Consuela doesn't remember getting on the plane to leave Madrid some twenty years before.

It's all a blur now and there are very few landmarks left at the airport to remind her as she lands there with Max and Tayanna.

She did not hesitate to agree to have the young girl accompany them since she and Max had become quite close.

She admired Tayanna for wanting to follow up on her search for the "golden flute" of the Aztecs.

Max and Tayanna are excited to see the city and she feels equally so with a large sense of uncertainty.

After settling in and having small snacks called Tapas at a nearby café, they head for the Gran Via, the main shopping and nightlife street.

Although the hotel clerk had described it as having now become the Spanish Broadway, Consuela wanted them to see it and found it to be a very familiar sight. As the taxi driver slowed in the heavy traffic, she pointed out the buildings she remembered well.

She began with the Torre, the tower that was once the tallest building in Spain at thirty six floors and the Plaza del Callao with the art deco movie theatre.

She saw that there were now five modern new ones alongside the theatre, and finally the Edificio Grassy with its grand architecture and round corner and steeple. She smiled at the addition of the illuminated Rolex watch sign over the door.

The driver stopped at a street Consuela has directed him to away from the center of the city. She explains to Tayanna and Max that there's a special church there. Her thoughts are bittersweet as she remembers the day that she and Juan walked to church and they promised to love each other and soon marry.

It has been an emotional trip to her past life and she decides they have time to stop for a prayer

Max pointed out a couple nearby. "She reminds me of my mother. I can picture her walking these streets arm in arm with my father, but his face is a blur."

He almost bumps into a woman rushing toward them.

"Consuela, is that truly you? It's been years, but you look the same."

Recognizing the woman as one who had worked at the Garcia house, she acknowledges the greeting politely but cautiously.

"It's been a long time, Anna. How have you been?"

"Ah, the years of scrubbing floors have taken their toll. My knees hurt all the time. Is this nice looking young man your son and this pretty one your daughter?"

"This is my nephew, Max, and his friend Tayanna."

"Good to see you Consuela. "Shall I say hello to Juan and the others at the house. He still works there with me."

Consuela knows that Anna was aware of her relationship with Juan and tries to hide her interest at the mention of his name. She asks if anyone has married or has children. Feeling a flutter of anxiety until the list is complete, Consuela smiles as no mention has been made of Juan.

"Sorry to rush off, Anna, but we have an appointment."

After walking some steps away and confident Anna is out of sight, Consuela tells Max and Tayanna to walk ahead.

"I'll catch up. I want to see something in this shop window."

Her face reflected in the glass shows the tears flowing down her cheeks and a small glimmer of hope in her eyes.

Anna wastes no time getting back to the manor house with her choice gossip. Her knees no longer ache as she scurries through the halls to the kitchen.

"Guess who I saw?"

Juan draws close to listen when Consuela's name is mentioned. Hearing she had two children with her he asks, "So she's married?"

"I didn't ask, but she wore no wedding ring and she said he was her nephew and a friend of his, but you remember how she left here in a hurry."

Juan is determined to find out more but does not question Anna further.

Consuela wants to begin anew and not dwell on the past and the next morning suggests that they go to the Cathedral. Tayanna has brought a letter from Father Gabriel in Mexico City to a priest he knows at the Madrid Cathedral named Father Tomas.

He said that he knew the priest was interested in Spanish history and particularly with New Spain, or Mexico as it is known now.

Father Tomas seems like a quiet man to Tayanna. He has a sober demeanor, but he does smile when he reads the letter from Father Gabriel.

His smile widens and his eyes light up when Tayanna tells him about her dream and her search for the ancient flute. He appreciates the young girl's determination.

"It will be my pleasure to be your guide for the next few days. First of all we'll start with the collection at the museum right here in Madrid.

"Being very familiar with the Museo de Americo in Madrid, Father Tomas leads them through the collection of Pre-Columbian artifacts of the Mayan and Aztec cultures.

"Our main interest is here, the Tro-Cortesianus Codex."

They are gazing at a long strip of paper with folds and drawings of the many everyday scenes they had seen depicted throughout the museum from hunting and handmade crafts to bloody images of human sacrifice.

"It was drawn on paper from the bark of fig trees and the subjects of the drawings differ from their knowledge of astronomy to times for planting crops. If folded up it would measure about nine inches by four and a half inches.

"There is another Mayan Codex in Dresden, Germany, but this is the one you might be most interested in.

"Two paper fragments added to the first and last pages are in Spanish writing. This has led to a belief that a Franciscan missionary may have added those words.

"The Codex came to the museum in two parts. The first was owned by Juan Tro y Ortolano and was found in the 1860's. The other part came to the museum in 1872 from Max Ignacio Miro, a book collector. He claimed that he got it in Extremadura, a province from which Hernan Cortes and other Conquistadores went to New Spain.

"Cortes is well known as the Conqueror of the natives of New Spain.

"A prophecy of the Aztec God Quexalcotl led Montezuma to believe that Hernan Cortes was the 'white skinned bearded God who would arrive from the East.'

"His ship landed on the coast in February and he arrived in the Aztec capitol on April twenty-second, the Day of Quexalcotl, at the end of the 'thirteenth heavens' and the beginning of the nine hells.' Accordingly, Montezuma greeted Cortes royally and showered him with many gifts."

Father Tomas went on, "Perhaps the museum had in mind the thought that Cortes brought the codex to Spain when they named it the Tro-Cortesianus Codex."

Tayanna has been listening closely and has been having a hard time containing her excitement. She is sure that somehow this is a clue to finding the flute.

"Father Tomas, how do we get to Extremadura and will you please take us there? I feel it's an important clue to finding the flute."

"Extremadura is a remote area of Spain bordering Portugal with mountains, forests, lakes and Roman ruins and Father Tomas smiles, "it is on my list of places to explore."

It's been a long drive the next day and Father Tomas suggests they spend the night at the Parador de Siguenza, one of the beautiful old castles in Spain that has been turned into a hotel and now welcomes visitors.

Nearby is a pilgrimage site to the Shrine of the Virgin Mary at the Royal Monastery of Santa Maria de Guadalupe. Since this is the place that Father Tomas had planned to visit for some time, he asks that they go to the Shrine to pay their respects the next morning.

It is a Franciscan Monastery and he's pleased when one of the monks notices his collar and greets him.

"Welcome, Father. I am Brother Pablo.

"Would you like me to escort you and your guests?"

Tayanna whispers to Father Tomas, "Ask him if Cortes brought home any artifacts from Mexico."

Father Tomas answers with a pointed finger to his pursed lips, but Tayanna's plea was already heard.

Brother Pablo smiles and does indulge her youthful enthusiasm but hopes that the priest hasn't brought tourists looking for souvenirs to take home.

"The history of Hernan Cortes is well known here but as for artifacts brought back from New Spain, you would have to speak with grandfather who often tells stories related to those times."

The young monk leads them to a garden where an older man is kneeling pulling weeds from a flower bed. His wrinkled face and white hair belie the youthful grace of his legs as he stands to greet them.

"Grandfather, our guests would hear the stories of the conquistadors that went to the new world and returned with lots of souvenirs." His tone is now not quite as cordial.

The old man's voice is soft and his tone is gentle.

"Brother Pablo means no disrespect. He is comfortable in these surroundings, but does reflect on the past and has serious thoughts on the future of our world."

"That's true. Grandfather repeats stories of ancient victories and violence that have been passed down from generation to generation.

"However, I fear that the lessons learned from those words fall on deaf ears. We hear terrible reports of violence forming every day that our children may be telling their grandchildren about some day. The cycle is proving difficult to break."

"THAT IS MY VERY CONCERN. THERE SEEMS TO BE NO END TO THE CYCLE OF REPETITION.

"YEARS OF WAR HAVE BEEN MIRRORED TIME AND AGAIN WITH THE ACCOMPANYING MISERY OF SO MANY INNOCENT PEOPLE."

"I cannot disagree with you about wars and the ensuing miseries of the people, even to your point of my reign and perhaps rethinking the victory at Troy, but this young monk seems to have come to the conclusion that our world may not be worth saving."

"I did not intend to make light of your visit and intentions. Our Grandfather, who is mine not by blood but by respect, enjoys telling of years gone by. People come from afar to listen to him. Please feel free to ask him your questions."

Max has been listening intently. He pokes Tayanna in the ribs. "This is your chance. Speak up."

His little push is like a shot of adrenaline. The words came quickly now to Tayanna beginning with the first dream, the trip to the museums in Mexico City and in Madrid, about the Monastery in Cuernavaca, the volcano at Popocatepetl, and now the Monastery here.

Taking a deep breath and trying hard not to cry she continues, "I feel strongly that the flute belongs in Mexico City and thought it might be somewhere in Spain, maybe even here in Extremadura.

"I want to right the wrong that was done to that little boy in my dream."

"Dry your eyes, child. Your quest is a worthy one and it has led you to all the right places, including your journey to Extremadura, but there may still be an obstacle in your way.

"I need some time to meditate on the proper path. Brother Pablo will find you in Madrid."

They all exchange a glance of bewilderment, including Brother Pablo, as the old man turns and heads for the shrine indicating an end to their conversation.

Elated with the possibilities and at the same time disappointed at the delay, they return to spend the night at the Parador before leaving for Madrid.

Max has been impressed with Father Tomas and how helpful he's been and that evening he asks him about his childhood and why he chose to become a priest.

He has already mentioned that he is now an orphan since his father died before he was born and his mother has now passed away. Father Tomas understands the boy's feelings of loneliness and tells him about his own life.

"My mother died when I was very young, too young to remember her. My father lives in Madrid and is quite wealthy.

"We've never been close and he did not approve of my taking vows.

"Most of my childhood was spent away at school. My brother Alvaro is much older and we grew up apart. He's been kind to me but he serves in the Army and is presently in Afghanistan with the NATO forces."

Stunned by the priest's words, Consuela stares at him closely to verify her thoughts and finds a moment later to be alone with him.

Her eyes are filled with tears. "You obviously don't remember me and I did not recognize you as a grown man.

Emilio, I cared for you from the day you were born until I left for America when you were five years old. I was your nanny. You were my little Emilio and I loved you."

His thoughts are whirling, Father Tomas doesn't remember Consuela, but he has heard many stories about the maid that his brother made pregnant.

"I am indeed Emilio Garcia. So Max is really your son by my brother Alvaro?"

"Oh, no. He is not my son. He is not even my nephew, but he is your brother's child and your nephew. You must see the resemblance to Alvaro and his green eyes match your own and your mother's.

Consuela quickly adds, "I'm sorry Emilio but we cannot tell him. He is a stable, congenial young man and I do love him as a son. He seeks information about his dead father which he will not be able to find.

"Since there was no reply to the letter I sent to your father saying his grandson would be coming to Madrid, I must assume that he would not be welcome into the family.

"I fear he would be hurt further."

"I fear you are right. I have never felt welcome in his home myself. However I am content with the life I have chosen and will help Max in any way I can. We'll speak about this again when we return to Madrid."

Meanwhile in Madrid, Juan is bringing breakfast to Don Alejandro. After setting the silver tray down, he confronts his patron in a tone he's never used in his presence before.

"I understand that Consuela and a young man from America she calls nephew are in Madrid.

"I would like to know what she had to say for herself in the letter you received."

"Ah, Juan. That scheming woman took my money for all these years and now she brings the bastard child to Madrid."

"So you have been always been in touch with her. Did she never ask about me?"

"You know I've always taken care of you. You belong here, not in America.

"I tore up her letters and she finally stopped writing. It was all for your own good."

Juan stands very stiffly and speaks in a restrained voice, although he feels he has been betrayed and wants to shout.

"I hereby give you my notice, Don Alejandro. I will leave the house immediately and not return.

I cannot work for a man who deceived me for so many years, a man who discarded his young son Emilio who is pure in heart and deed and rewarded the one who did not act honorably and shamed the family.

"You violated my trust and treated Consuela and Maria poorly, not to mention your only grandson. May God have mercy on you."

Don Alejandro's cheeks are red. He begins to rebuke Juan, but a maid's knock on the door interrupts them.

"My apologies, Don Alejandro. There are two Army officers here. They are asking to see you. I have shown them to the Library."

DESTINY

The officers have come with the terrible news that Don Alejandro's eldest son, Alvaro, has been killed in Afghanistan.

The kind words of his son's heroism in the line of duty do nothing to alleviate his anguish and grief. Don Alejandro falls to the floor of the library when he hears the news. The doctor is called and Don Alejandro is given a sedative and put to bed.

Juan hurries to the Cathedral to tell Emilio the sad news of the death of his brother.

When told that Father Tomas is away, he leaves a note with the news of Alvaro. He adds his condolences and promises to send details of the funeral arrangements.

Juan cannot bring himself to abandon Don Alvarez at this time.

The army officials sent word that Alvaro's body has been flown to Madrid and, since Emilio could not be reached, Juan makes arrangements for the funeral service to be held at the Cathedral.

Hearing of his brother's untimely death on arriving back in Madrid on the eve of the funeral, Father Tomas prays for a long time and makes a decision to follow his heart.

He tells Consuela that his brother has been killed and asks if she will allow Max to attend.

"Emilio, I cannot tell him the truth myself but I cannot deny him attending his father's funeral. God plays a big part in all our lives, and I know it is the right thing."

"I believe she means to give you credit for all the good things in life, but then you must receive credit for some bad things as well."

"The old man should receive a punishment for his deeds, but it's my understanding that no matter how evil, all will be forgiven."

"YOU ARE NOT WRONG IN YOUR BELIEF OF FORGIVENESS BUT ALL WRONG DOINGS HAVE AN EFFECT ON THE PERPETRATOR.

"THE ONE YOU CALL OLD MAN HAS TURNED HIS HEART HARD FOR MANY YEARS AND HAS HAD VERY LITTLE LOVE OR HAPPINESS IN HIS LIFE."

The Spanish flag is draped over the dark mahogany casket in front of the altar.

Flower arrangements of many sizes and shapes flow across from one side of the church to the other.

Juan had made sure to notify many of the dignitaries that Don Alejandro associated with the upper classes and they had come to honor the fallen soldier. Government officials, officers of the army as well as men he served with, and representatives of NATO stood along with the servants from the Garcia household to mourn the loss of Alvaro.

In his grief, Don Alejandro struggles to remain composed as many rise to pay homage to his son. Father Tomas, dressed in simple vestments, tells a few anecdotes from their childhood.

Consuela has brought Max and Tayanna to attend the funeral of Father Tomas brother without divulging anything more. Seeking anonymity, she leads them to a pew near the door and shrinks back at the sight of Juan at Don Alejandro's side.

"Today we shed tears for my brother Alvaro's passing…"

Father Tomas pauses and then continues while raising his right arm in the direction of the back of the church. "and now we must also shed tears of joy that his son has come to us. Let us rejoice and welcome him with open arms."

Consuela is frightened but tells Max to go to Father Tomas. Moving forward slowly, Max is confused by the words of Father Tomas and the stares confronting him.

He does not understand what's happening.

A grey haired old man is coming toward him crying out, "Oh, my God. My Alvaro is alive. They made a big mistake. Someone else is in that coffin."

Don Alejandro heads for Max with his arms outstretched and falters as he reaches for him and sees his green eyes. Juan rushes to his side and lowers him to the ground and then turns toward the boy.

"Yes, he does look just like his father."

Juan's eyes, however, quickly move in another direction as he sees Consuela rushing to the young man that looks like Alvaro.

Father Tomas asks everyone to remain calm and to clear the aisle for the doctor, who is already coming forward. Don Alejandro opens his eyes and Father Tomas leans down to whisper to him.

"This is your time, father. You must embrace your grandson now in God's house and forgive yourself for abandoning the child. I know that God will forgive you, as Alvaro's son will.

"I have chosen the church and have no need of titles or money.

"Max is the rightful heir to your name and all that you will leave behind in this life."

Don Alejandro searches the green eyes of the son he has ignored for so long knowing that he is right to condemn his actions.

There are tears in his own eyes as the realization reaches him. Here before him is a young man with the face and blood of his son Alvaro and the green eyes of his beloved wife, Emilia and his son Emilio.

Tayanna sat down slowly in the pew when Father Tomas beckoned Max forward and stayed there as Consuela rushed down the aisle.

"So the funeral is for Max's father who wasn't dead, but is dead now. Who's the old man that fainted? Why is Consuela crying and why is that man holding her in his arms? I'm very happy for Max, but this is so confusing. Now Max is hugging Father Tomas and he's crying too. I better go help Max."

Brother Pablo had entered the church and remained in back when he saw that a funeral was taking place. He too was confused by what transpired and is waiting patiently to see Father Tomas.

Consuela introduces Juan to Tayanna and Max. "He is very dear to me and I know he will be most helpful to Max in his new life here in Spain."

"I don't know what to say about my new life, but I know I don't want you to leave Tayanna."

"I'm glad to hear that, Max. You know the Madrid Symphony Orchestra may have scholarships to study here. I understand it was founded in 1903 and one of the earliest members, Francisco Gonzalez, played the flute."

"I must thank you, Tayanna. You have been a good friend to Max when he needed one and I'm not sure we even would have come back to Spain. Your quest became our quest and Max now knows his true past and has a bright future.

"You have helped him find his uncle and now my true love Juan and I will continue our lives together."

"We have much to thank you for." adds Juan.

Brother Pablo has come up to the group quietly.

"You cannot leave yet, Tayanna. Your quest has not been concluded.

"After much contemplation and prayer, Grandfather has convinced the sisters at the convent where the flute was kept out of sight that it should be returned to Mexico as a symbol of friendship. He said we should learn from our mistakes of the past and make amends.

"I must confess that I was mistaken when I assumed that you were seeking the valuable flute for selfish reasons. Grandfather knew at once that you had a higher purpose and that the flute would have a special significance for you.

"He has asked me to bring it here to show you first and then to travel to Mexico and have it placed in the Museum where the Sun Stone is displayed.

"Would you like to see what you have gone to so much trouble to find?"

"Yes, I too would like to see the bejeweled flute that has sent us traveling around the world."

"PATIENCE, ZEUS, PATIENCE.

With everyone around her, Tayanna takes a box from Brother Pablo.

She is surprised as she holds the box in her hands and very gently opens the lid.

It is not the flute of her dreams!

"Why, it looks so old and so crudely made. There are no jewels, no gold ornamentation."

For a moment she thinks there's been a big mistake and she is sorely disappointed.

Suddenly she hears the music of the flute and thinks back to the face of the boy that she saw playing it as the Conquistador rode toward him.

He was about ten years old, barefoot, and his clothes were simple.

She now realizes that he looked like he worked in the fields, a lot like one of the kids she grew up with. She looks around at her friends with tears in her eyes.

"It's made of wood, just like the magic flute that my father carved for me."

POSEIDON

THE PAST IS PROLOGUE

"I UNDERSTAND IN ONE MYTHICAL STORY PROMETHEUS STOLE FIRE FROM YOU AND GAVE IT TO MAN. YOU GOT EVEN BY HAVING A WOMAN SENT TO HIM THAT WAS MADE FROM THE MUD OF THE EARTH."

"As the god in charge, I could certainly not ignore his insolence."

"SO IN REVENGE YOU SENT HIM THE WOMAN PANDORA WHO BROUGHT PLAGUE, DISEASE AND SORROW TO THE WORLD."

"Not so fast. Remember your free will theory. They were all sealed in a jar with strict instructions not to open it.

"Pandora represented temptation, and so it was by choice that these evils were loosed by man upon himself. Man was just lucky that Hope was also included."

"HERE WE ARE IN GREECE BY THE BEAUTIFUL AEGEAN SEA. WAS IT NOT SAID THAT ONE OF YOUR GODS SANK 'THE LOST CITY' OF ATLANTIS?

"Well, the name of Poseidon does come to mind."

"I UNDERSTAND IT IS BELOW THE SEA SOMEWHERE NEARBY. BUT AGAIN THIS IS A MYTHICAL STORY DEVISED BY PLATO THE PHILOSOPHER WHO WROTE MANY WORDS ABOUT THE NATURE OF MAN.

"HE SPOKE OF HOW CIVILIZATIONS CLAIMING PERFECTION IN THEIR CHOICE OF GOVERNMENT WOULD GO TO WAR TO DEFEND THEIR POLITICAL POSITIONS AGAINST ANY CULTURE THAT DEVIATED.

"OR WAS IT PERHAPS THEIR RELIGIOUS DEVOTION TO DIFFERENT GODS THAT LED TO THE DESTRUCTION OF ATLANTIS, THE CIVILIZATION THAT PLATO DESCRIBED AS A HIGHLY ADVANCED CULTURAL MARVEL OF ARCHITECTURE AND ENGINEERING."

"The people of Atlantis were corrupt and greedy and the gods simply decided their culture had to go. Poseidon and his mighty waves of water might have played some part in the disaster."

"SO YOU PLACE THE BLAME ON YOUR DAUGHTER'S RIVAL.

"DID ATHENA COME TO YOU IN FEAR THAT POSEIDON'S MIGHTY STRIKE TO THE EARTH THAT BROUGHT FORTH WATER WOULD PROVE MORE POPULAR IN THEIR CONTEST THAN HER SIMPLE OLIVE TREE?"

"Peace and prosperity came to the people along with the seed of the olive tree when they chose Athena the winner and worshipped her."

"AH ZEUS, WOULD THAT AN OLIVE BRANCH MIGHT HAVE THE SAME EFFECT TODAY."

"If, as you say, Poseidon is a myth, then he is no longer here to stir the waters and send tsunami waves to end rival civilizations that insist on war to reconcile their differences. Perhaps that task is now left up to you."

"I INDULGE YOU ONCE MORE AND REMIND YOU THAT YOU ARE AS MUCH A MYTH AS POSEIDON."

Zeus brings the subject back to their mission and avoids the insinuation.

"You mention my Athena and I remind you that you have promised not to intrude on the thoughts of the mortal Athena arriving in Greece today."

"I SHALL KEEP MY WORD."

"Yasou, cousin. Welcome to Athens."

Athena's cousin Spiro greets her as she comes through the door from the customs area at the airport.

He'd been to visit her home in America several times and she's glad to see his familiar face.

Conversation flows easily as they drive from the airport into the city. "How do your studies go? Your mother mentioned you are going to be a nurse."

"Yes, but I've only started. At first it will be book knowledge and then the real thing. I really want to work with children. So many require hospital stays and nursing care is important."

"I understand that now you want to go island hopping like a tourist."

"Well, I must go to Delos. My father insists since the twin gods Apollo and Artemis were born there. He still regrets naming me Athena and my brother, George.

"The myths of the ancient Greeks are a very important part of Greek history according to my father."

Zeus beams.

"She is perfect. Her thoughts are pure. She brings joy to my heart. I must help her."

"WHY ARE YOU MUTTERING? DO YOU WISH ME TO WASH MY THOUGHTS OF THIS ATHENA OR NOT?"

"The most important island I want to visit is Lesvos. There are so many conflicting reports as to what goes on there with all the migrants. I want to see for myself."

"Your Aunt Sophia wants to spoil you for a few days first. She made all the special dishes you liked so much when you were here some years ago. You were a little girl with a big stomach and she loved filling it."

Aunt Sophia welcomes them with a table set in the garden overflowing with Athena's favorites.

"We can do some sightseeing in Athens, but the ancient relics have not changed much," Spiro muses.

"When I was here for the Olympics in 2004, the one thing that stuck in my memory was the Parthenon.

"Even though it was in ruins and not perfect I was thrilled to be there. Whenever it came up at school, I very proudly stood and said that I was actually there."

"Athena, you must be tired. It's time to rest now. I've made up a bed for you on the couch."

"Thank you, Aunt Sophia. It was a long trip."

The Parthenon that Athena dreams of that night is perfect. All the Doric style columns are intact and the roof is complete just like in the schoolbooks of her youth. It's not like the ruins she remembers on her visit.

There are no people walking up the hill towards the building alongside her. She remembered the first time that crowds of tourists were busy taking pictures, jostling for a good view.

Now there are five women coming down the hill slowly from the Parthenon. They are dressed in long gowns similar to the prom dress her mother had made.

"Good day, Athena. We are the granddaughters of Apollo. We are here to greet you," the first girl begins. "My name is Hygieia and I bring health."

"My name is Iaso, and I bring medicine."

"I am Aceso and I do my best to heal."

The fourth woman has red cheeks.

"As you can see, I bring a healthy color. I am Aglaea."

The last girl is the tallest and seems to glow. "My name is Panacea, the universal remedy."

"Why are we here alone at the Parthenon?"

"The Parthenon is dedicated to the patron of our city, Athena. We are the goddesses of Healing.

"It has become known to us that you have been sent to help the world to heal and you will begin with the people on the island of Lesvos who need you."

"Thank you, ladies. I know this Athena can do it. She is so far above the others."

The next morning at breakfast, Athena does not tell her dream. "It seemed so real, but was too silly to mention."

"I have to work this week, Athena, but Tasos is set to tour with you. He knows the islands well and will be glad for something to do. He finished at the University and is a doctor now, but there are no openings at hospitals, no money to start your own service, and no other work for that matter.

"Our country's economy, like so many others, is struggling to keep up with the major players.

After another day indulging Aunt Sophia and worrying about her expanding waistline, Athena and Cousin Spiro's son Tasos take a ferry from the port of Piraeus to the island of Mykonos.

Tasos had suggested they spend some time in Mykonos since it was the "party island" and appealed to the club scene participants. He was pleased when Athena declined and wanted to go straight on to Delos.

"I'm impressed. You're not just a tourist after all. So many times these islands are sought for pure hedonistic pleasure.

"Delos is a sacred center and was once a very important city.

"It was a busy duty free port and trading was ongoing with the Syrians and Egyptians for over five hundred years.

"It is still a very special place, a sacred treasure of antiquities for anyone interested in seeing the concrete statues of what many call the mythical gods.

"Now there are only a few residents, fourteen at the last census, and no one is allowed to spend the night.

"What a beautiful introduction to the island. My eyes water."

"I DO NOT DISAGREE ABOUT ITS BEAUTY, BUT SUGGEST THE SEA MIST HAS GOTTEN TO YOUR EYES."

After a half hour ride in a smaller boat, they arrive at the Sacred Harbour of Delos.

They head first to the Sanctuary of Apollo and then go a little further to that of Artemis.

Athena takes photos of every angle of both on her cell phone anticipating her father's request.

"The stone lions are still intact, but many statues have heads missing. How come, Tasos?"

"The lions look so good because they've been redone. The missing heads are no surprise.

"Some might have been taken by looters, but any new religion appearing anywhere throughout time made it a practice to either eradicate the old or change it so that it would be forgotten."

"Indeed, it was terrible to watch my civilization crumbling piece by piece. Do we credit you with that idea?"

"ANCIENT RELIGIONS USED IDOLS TO CENTER THE THOUGHTS OF THE PEOPLE. YOU CAN SEE EXAMPLES IN MANY MUSEUMS.

"CHIPPING STONES TO CREATE A FACE AND A BODY GAVE THE BEHOLDER A FOCAL POINT TO SEE AND TOUCH. SMALL FIGURINES OF ODD SHAPES OF THE HUMAN FIGURE AND PARTS OF ANIMALS WERE EASILY CARRIED IN NOMADIC TIMES AND DREW PEOPLE TOGETHER IN A SETTING OF WORSHIP.

"CAVE DRAWINGS OF PICTURES WERE TURNED INTO STORIES THAT HOLY MEN INTERPRETED AS THEY SAW FIT. SINCE PRIESTS WERE THE FIRST TO LEARN TO READ AND WRITE THEY OFTEN USED SIGNS AND EVENTS TO SOLVE LOCAL PROBLEMS AND SECURE THEIR POWER USING FEAR."

"So I guess that's the basis for the first two 'thou shalt nots' in the bible. Mortals shall only worship you and absolutely no idols."

"IT'S A LONG CLIMB UP TO THE TOP OF MOUNT MYNTHOS.

"THE VIEW IS SPECTACULAR, WHY DON'T YOU KEEP YOUR MIND ON THAT?"

Athena also appreciates the view. "I don't know what's more gratifying, Tasos. The statues are beautiful, but they don't hold a candle to the view. This is really God's work."

God smiles.

Tasos and Athena stop at the Sacred Lake where Leto gave birth to the twins. The twins were then hidden for fear that Hera, Zeus' jealous wife, would harm them."

"I feel some affinity to this place. Knowing they were twins and children of the god Zeus gives me goose bumps. Silly thoughts run through my head at times."

"That's the right of every woman, cousin, and why we men don't really understand them."

"You sound like my good friend, Michael."

"Is that a serious friendship, leading to an engagement to marry?"

"That sounds like something my mother or yours would ask. I wouldn't tell them anything because they would push the romance along, but I'll tell you. It's way too soon and both of us have a lot we want to do, but maybe some time in the future.

"I know I'm going to become a nurse and right now, I'm enjoying my Greek heritage. Tomorrow we head for Lesvos and more pressing matters."

"Should I worry about the relationship between my Athena and Michael," thought Zeus.

"SHOULD I WORRY ABOUT THE RELATIONSHIP BETWEEN MY MICHAEL AND ATHENA?

"That was quite a long ferry ride, Tasos. I did not realize how close Lesvos is to Turkey. Why it's right there. You can see it clearly."

"You're right Athena. Lesvos lies within sight of Turkey, some three or four miles across the narrow Mytilini Strait in some places.

"But don't be fooled by the beautiful calm sea today. Hundreds of asylum seekers have drowned in that narrow stretch of water.

"Those inflatable boats used by the illegal traders and meant for fifteen are overloaded by forty people and sit very low in the water, making them vulnerable to even minor weather disturbances.

"The normal island population is eighty six thousand, with a third of the people living in the capital, Mytilene, in the southern part of the island. The rest of the people are scattered over the island.

"Just three years ago, over one million migrants seeking refuge landed on the shores of this small island and they keep coming. Most of the migrants still on the island are in the northern part."

Athena and Tasos decide to go to Molyvos at the northern tip of the island. They have been told that the holding center for migrants called Moria is near there.

An old man is sitting in the sun by his boat mending his fishing nets and greets them.

"Kali merra, pethya." Good day, Children.

"Good day to you, Papou."

"He can't fool me, that's Poseidon. What does he want now?"

"My name is Tasos. My cousin Athena and I were just looking around and saw the field of discarded lifejackets. I suppose they are from the many migrants in the Moria camp."

"Old man, I know who you are. Are you here to make trouble for my Athena?"

The old man replies to Zeus. The private thought waves between them are strong.

"My fish are diminishing, the waters of the sea are polluted and my dolphins whisper fears in my ear. We have the problem of the immigrants here on this small island, but this is minor compared to the devastation of my pure waters.

"If Athena has the answer to any of my problems, she is most welcome."

"We are in agreement on the problems of the oceans and I understand and share your frustration in being unable to instigate changes in the unstable actions of the mortals.

"The mortal Athena has many of the attributes of a goddess.

"It would not surprise me to learn that she may help mankind."

The exchange has taken place in seconds and the old man answers Tasos.

"Ah yes, the Moria Camp is just down the road. You know it was built to hold three thousand and now they house over six thousand. There are many more migrants camped here and there with no covering over their heads.

"Athena, you are a young girl. Go and help at the house up on the hill. The women are preparing hundreds of sandwiches and soon the line will be long at the door.

"But first you and your cousin will sit and keep me company while I tell of the old Lesvos."

"IT IS DIFFICULT TO DESCRIBE LESVOS SINCE THEIR CULTURE HAS UNDERGONE CHANGE MANY TIMES"

"Poseidon may enlighten us today. Lesvos held a small place in the ancient world. It was not a very memorable place to me."

"Many, many years ago when Greece was not called Greece and Turkey was not called Turkey, and there were glaciers changing the shape of our world, Lesvos was separated from the mainland."

The old man continues, "Although a very small part of the world, Lesvos once was a city-state, was plundered by raids from Venice, has been taken over by Rome, ruled by a Turkish Emir and invaded by Ottoman Turks. It finally became a part of Greece during the Balkan War in 1912.

"It is hard to describe the culture of the people of Lesvos today. They have managed to handle the chaos when anti-immigration policies and lack of willingness to share the burden left them to handle this crisis that has hit the island."

"Perhaps that's why the island of Lesvos is the perfect landing place for the lost souls who try to conquer the ocean.

"The culture has been turned over and over for generations and the heart beats of the people are universal and open to welcoming those in need.

"Even the men cry at the sight of the dead babies carried in by the tide and the women run to swaddle them with their shawls."

"YOU DO ACTUALLY UNDERSTAND MY WORLD SOMETIMES."

Tasos is impressed with the knowledge of the old man.

"You know more of the world than most. It is a pleasure to meet you. Thank you for the lesson."

Athena looks into the old man's eyes. She sees the weariness of his aging and the worry for his children and grandchildren. There is also room for worry for his neighbors, the migrants.

"Yes, Papou. Thank you. And I will gladly help make the sandwiches. I am not a nurse as yet, but I'm sure that there are many more things I can do."

The old man motions to a young girl passing, "Panacea, show Athena where the women are. She wants to help."

WHAT IF

Michael is President of the Astronomy Club and is presiding at their weekly meeting.

"My talk today is about the Past, Present and Future of the Universe. We are embarking on careers in Science.

"One very interesting Law of Physics points out the present state of our world in precise language.

"The definition of the State of Entropy is often given as 'lacking order or predictability, a gradual decline into disorder,' and many times used with synonyms such as 'deterioration' or 'chaos.'

"Globalization has presented problems by increasing complexity and uncertainty, but like Alice in Wonderland's magnifying glass that distorts out of proportion it can also bring things into more clear perspective.

"It is clear. Mankind has failed with almost every decision we've made.

"We decided at the onset that we could not live in harmony. Although we'd been given ample fish, fowl, plants, animals and water to share, if anyone reached for what we considered 'ours' it meant war.

"If someone trespassed on what we deemed our piece of the Earth, or if we wanted what someone else claimed, again war was the answer. One clansman killed might mean thousands killed in revenge.

"It seems that like black holes in the Universe, man has a place in his mind for black thoughts and is unable to stop himself from going there.

"At this moment many countries around the globe are involved in, or at the brink of, a state of war."

"MICHAEL BRINGS SATISFACTION TO MY MIND FOR HE SPEAKS MY THOUGHTS."

"He is rather interesting to listen to. For one so young, he speaks in the profound way of prophets and Greek philosophers."

"ZEUS, YOUR THOUGHTS ARE SOUND TODAY. YOU SEEM TO BE LEARNING AT A BETTER PACE THAN OUR STUDENTS."

Zeus keeps his next thought to himself.

"My only concern is Michael's interest in Athena. He follows her too closely and she accepts his attention gladly.

"There is no chance for her to seek a prince of her stature, or at the least a man of great wealth and power."

"There is a God," Michael continues.

"Many of you have doubts, but God lives in every fiber of each one of you.The Earth was developed by the will of God over millions of years using various parts of the Universe.

"Man was formed as an integral part of that Universe. Once established, the Earth needed Man to maintain it and, at a crucial point, the Holy Spirit and Jesus were needed to correct an imbalance that was affecting the nature and future of Mankind.

"INDEED, I DID TAKE THE IMBALANCE OF GOOD BEING OVERCOME BY BAD FORCES INTO MY CALCULATIONS THAT A CHANGE WAS NEEDED."

"You rub salt into my wounds, however the need for change is becoming clear to me."

The audience is intrigued.

"The holy trinity is really a multi-linity. We are all connected. The DNA of the Earth is the DNA of man and the chain of man is multi-faceted. There are sharp edges in the chain and there are also smooth sections.

"There are tangles that must be worked out for the chain to survive.

"We are here at the will of God, but keep in mind that he handed that will to us, free will for man to make his own decisions.

"MICHAEL TAKES MY INSTRUCTIONS AS MY HOLY SPIRIT SERIOUSLY. I MUST MAKE SURE ZEUS DOES NOT INTERFERE WITH HIM.

"HE SWORE NOT TO, BUT THEN JUDITH AND ATHENA ARE PRESENT AND HE HAS AN EXCUSE TO EAVESDROP."

"Man plays a big part in the art of balance. It follows that man must now overcome the prejudices and imbalances that prevail today.

"Skin is but a thin layer of different colors covering our bodies, which have identical hearts and souls. At some point man decided that skin color defined your place in the universe, not realizing that man's actions are placed on the scales and that true balance is necessary for the Earth to continue to exist and avoid extinction.

"Now he sounds like he is preaching your gospel, or some pie-eyed version of it. What does skin have to do with balance?"

"YOU MAY CONSIDER THAT YOU ARE WHITE. HOWEVER, NO PARTICULAR COLOR CAN CLAIM ME.

"I REFLECT THE COLOR OF PEOPLE, ALL OF THEM. MY SKIN IS MANY SHADES FROM

WHITE TO BLACK AND MY EYES ARE BLUE, GRAY, BLACK, BROWN, AND GREEN

"THEY MAY SLANT UPWARDS, DOWNWARDS, OR NOT AT ALL. IN OTHER WORDS, IN BALANCE.

"BUT MICHAEL'S THOUGHTS ARE OF MORE INTEREST AT THE MOMENT."

"Many books have been written about the problems plaguing Earth at this time and the doom and gloom that will befall us if we do not stop adding to our population or learning to grow food more quickly.

"Modern technology attempts to accomplish this, but disease will follow in the wake of additives and pesticides used to reach that goal.

"People are aging more slowly with the aid of medical chemicals, however many will be lost in the halls of nursing homes and the dreams of drugs.

"The sea is threatening to overtake low lying areas around the globe and at the same time many parts of the earth are parched and water is scarce.

"Proposals to rebuild our waterfronts and to limit use to conserve water are met with financial skepticism and political blocking.

"Now let us take a peek at the past.

"In 1791 Thomas Jefferson had the process of desalinizing water printed and placed on board every ship. It was a tedious process using boiler steam.

"Today, with modern methods, a gallon of desalinated water costs .004 cents. If we figure the cost of bottled water at single bottles, which most people use, the cost for bottled water is a little under eight dollars per gallon.

"WHAT IF the world chose to have more researchers working to solve the problem rather than paying excessive amounts for bottled water?

"Some countries are rushing to put up walls to keep the foreigners out because they're taking the jobs and causing the problems, but the walls have been leaking for too long and cannot hold.

"Let's keep playing the game of "WHAT IF."

"Around 400 BC in the Greek City of Taras, a man named General Archytas, a close friend of Plato the philosopher, constructed a bird and used steam to power the movements of his wooden robot.

"He did this as a hobby but he was most famous as a general, mostly for never having lost a battle.

"Actually, my god of fire and metal work Hephaestus made mechanical robots at his forge on Mt. Olympus.

"He had automatons that worked for him including tripods that could walk. Why he even used one as a guide dog for blind Orion."

"SURE, SURE, IN YOUR MYTHS. LET THE BOY CONTINUE."

"WHAT IF General Archytas was not given the order to leave home and fight the enemy but instead given a grant to build a better robot in 400 BC?

"WHAT IF we had heeded the direction of God as given to Isaiah and 'beat our swords into plowshares and our spears into pruning hooks.'

"In 1495, Leonardo DaVinci published designs for a mechanical knight which led to the manufacture of mechanical toy knights.

"When the Westinghouse Company built the Televox Robot in 1927, many more minds turned to researching and developing computers and robots.

"WHAT IF before the beginning of World War Two in the early forties, we could have had the use of robots to fight and the blood of sixty million people would not have been shed.

"Abraham Lincoln once said, 'A house divided against its self cannot stand.'

"He was talking about the United States which covers less than two percent of the Earth's surface. Our country was fairly new but had global ties which led to slavery being brought to the New World. Slavery was not unique. In fact it had been around in General Archytas time.

"WHAT IF technological advances had been given priority over war and we had robots.

"WHAT IF we had overcome the temptation to use our fellow man as slaves?

"Before the Civil War, were there enough men looking for options and solutions, or were most cleaning their rifles and preparing to defend their position at all costs.

"WHAT IF we were faced with similar temptations today?

"Do we choose war, do we enslave others? Do we reinforce poverty and starvation by neglect?

"Do we remember Lincoln's admonition?

"Right now you're all thinking what the hell does this have to do with Astronomy. After all this is a meeting of the Astronomy Club.

"While studying Astronomy, we are reviewing our past course in the vast Universe and what our future course might be. We are not limited to what we can see in the sky above us."

"Now he sounds like one of the Greek poets that kept crowds interested with their tall stories and theories. A bit strange, but the girl Judith follows and listens closely. Her thoughts come through clearly."

"Athena, his words are like a beacon of light. He's not like any other man I know. He's the only one who didn't laugh when I told him how Jesus carried me out of the car crash that killed my parents. Michael is an angel. He's the angel of God."

God's thoughts are guarded.

"SHE HAS NO IDEA HOW CLOSE TO THE TRUTH THAT IS."

"Judith, don't get carried away. I think Michael is just being a little dramatic to keep everybody interested.

"He wanted a couple of friendly faces in the audience to insure some applause. He can be quite a ham. Thanks for coming with me."

Michael continues talking to the members of the Astronomy Club.

There was an announcement of the meeting in the school newspaper and the number of students usually attending has increased quite a bit.

"Let's not forget about the importance of our actions today and its effect on the future, but we cannot omit Mother Nature when discussing the past and future of the world.

"NASA's Earth Observatory lists cold and warm intervals in the past and gives the possible causes as cyclical lows in solar radiation, heightened volcanic activity, changes in oceanic circulation and variations in the Earth's orbit and axial tilt.

"Last year, 2018, has seen more than the usual number of major hurricanes, floods, volcanoes, wildfires, cyclones, wind and dust storms, and mudslides wiping out towns. Earthquakes wreaked havoc while demolishing whole cities, wildfires burned thousands of acres and many homes, and there was mass flooding."

"We might question Hades about the volcanic eruptions and Poseidon about the ocean's tsunami waves, and unless you have been messing with tilting the earth, I think the climate change deal falls on the shoulders of mankind.

"Or have you been messing around with floods again?"

God has no answer for Zeus. His thoughts are of admiration of Michael and his comments.

"There have been studies on the Planet Mars and its capability of becoming habitable for humans.

"At this point, only sources of water stand out as a big deterrent.

"The Space Telescope Science Institute that operates the Hubble Telescope for NASA and the European Space Industry stated in 2015 that Ceres is one of the tens of thousands of asteroids in the belt between Mars and Jupiter.

"It is the largest asteroid at about the size of Texas. Computer models suggest Ceres' core is of dense material with lighter material near the surface.

"The mantle is thought to be rich in icy water surrounding a rocky core. If that mantle is made up of at least twenty-five percent water, Ceres would have more water than Earth.

"NASA's planned mission, Mars 2020, is set to launch next year to investigate the origins, early evolution and the possibility of future life on Mars.

"And I think the debate about finding Martians there is finally over and we won't have to wage a war for it.

"Ha. So he does have a sense of humor."

"We may well end up using the resources of outer space to the Earth's advantage. God's influence is not limited to Earth.

"I am sure that our past choices are insurmountable and our future place in the Universe will be on Mars.

"There may well be an expedition in fifteen or twenty years and I will right now place my name on the list of volunteers to settle the new home of Man."

"Amazing, such charisma. That young man has me intrigued with his scheme. Perhaps his new world has a place for an experienced god."

"HIS SCHEME DOES OPEN UP MANY NEW AVENUES OF THOUGHT."

One of the members of the club has written a news report on Michael's talk for the school newspaper. Sitting in front of Judith during Michael's talk, he heard her rapt description of Michael and smiled.

"His description of doom and gloom for us unless we escape to Mars is fabulous. I can do a front page on this guy."

The cartoon of Michael with wings drawn and the description of him as the "Angel of the People" was shared on social media and spread quickly throughout the student community and out into the world. Facebook, Twitter and Instagram blew up.

Whether they take it as a joke or are actually interested in joining the expedition doesn't seem to matter. Michael is news.

It has been accepted by the news media as a viable story and the news anchor is serious in her questioning.

"Will you head up the expedition to settle Mars in ten years? More than twenty thousand young people are convinced we can reach Mars in ten years and have expressed an interest in going. Are you going to lead them?"

Watching in their dorm room, Judith jumps up. "Oh say yes, say yes. I'll go with you. His words are like a beacon of light that I must follow.

We'll get married, have kids and start a whole new world, just like Adam and Eve."

"GOOD. I CAN ADHERE TO MY OWN VOW NOT TO LOOK IN ON ATHENA BY LISTENING TO THIS ONE."

Athena laughs. "You're a nut, Judith. Nobody's going to Mars any time soon.

"That's just a bunch of scientists dreaming. Michael is sweet, but he'll get over this altruistic save-the-world phase he's in. He could become an astronaut, but that's about it."

"I am enjoying every moment of this. With all his speed Mercury could not have begun to spin this yarn so fast."

"ALTHOUGH IT MAY SEEM UNLIKELY THAT THIS COULD HAPPEN SO SOON, THE GRAIN OF THOUGHT IS IN HIS MIND AND HE HAS PUT IT INTO MINE.

"HIS PRESENCE ON EARTH MAY HAVE A GREATER SIGNIFICANCE THAN EITHER ONE OF US ANTICIPATED."

UNSETTLING CONFLICT

Back at school after the visit to his grandparents in West Virginia, Bill is in his dorm room getting ready to watch the video series on Viet Nam.

His visit had stirred interest in some things his mother had said and in his grandmother's birthplace. Most of all he kept thinking of his grandfather's words about how badly they had been treated when they came home.

He's always considered himself American, but there's a lot of talk on social media about ancestry, DNA and immigrants not being welcome and now he's curious. He'd heard talk at school about what a raw deal the Viet Nam veterans got when they arrived home and how they never should have been there in the first place.

There's a soft knock on the door and he's surprised and pleased to see Judith standing there.

"Hi, Bill. I'm surprised you aren't at the party with Athena. She told me she thought you'd be there.

"I thought maybe Michael could use some female company."

"Sorry, but it's just me. Michael's out somewhere and I'm getting ready to watch the Viet Nam War story on television."

"Well, I drove all this way. I guess I'll watch with you. Got any beer?"

With a couple of beers and a few pillows behind them they settle in against the wall on the top bunk.

Bill is pleased to be this close to Judith, but his thoughts are concentrated on the televised video, while Judith is disappointed at missing Michael but doesn't mind leaning on Bill's shoulder.

As the film unfolds, Bill's mind goes through various stages. He's proud of his own grandfather but he can't imagine him in the scenes with young soldiers throwing grenades and firing at people.

He gets quite upset when children that look so much like him are involved and suffering. He gets mad at the scenes showing Americans demonstrating against the war, but as the complications of the politics are stripped away, his anger turns to frustration.

"What would I have thought? I guess since I'm part Vietnamese, I would have pretty mixed emotions. Why would we be at a war with Vietnamese people? How was Cambodia involved? I never even heard of Cambodia.

"But if I was only American, would I volunteer to go fight in Vietnam?

"I think I would have gone if ordered to do so, but I'm not sure after seeing some of those disturbing scenes.

"Judith, I don't see what's changed.

"The wars keep going on. Another wall that will be built to honor those that died in Iraq and Afghanistan will have new names, but nothing else is different."

"He has to realize that war is part of the game of life and always has been."

"I THINK THIS YOUNG MAN IS OPENING HIS MIND TO NEW THINKING ALTHOUGH HE IS NOT YET SURE WHAT IT SHOULD BE."

"You're right, Bill. We do need change and you need to be part of the solution.

"Why don't you join me and my friends? We're making sure we're prepared to defend ourselves no matter what comes at us. We meet every Friday night at the gun range.

"Taking charge of our own lives is important and going to the other side of the world to fight a war is futile. The next one may well be on our doorstep. We can only take care of our country and our families if we're properly prepared.

"Do you know how to shoot an automatic rifle?"

"I FEAR THAT IS A PATH LEADING TO A DEAD END AND ONE THAT MANY ARE CHOOSING."

A week later, Bill is standing near the door listening. Judith is up on her desk making a speech to the twenty students crowded into her dorm room one Friday.

She's recruiting them to encourage others to vote to keep the Republican Conservatives in office in the 2018 Fall elections.

"We have to make sure that President Trump is re-elected in 2020 and that means no change in the status quo in Washington this year.

"There are a lot of Democrats out there trying to say that he somehow colluded with the Russians. We know that's a lie. President Trump himself said it was not true. Who are we to believe, our duly elected President or some loud mouthed liberals."

One of the students sitting on the floor begins to laugh and about half the group join in. A more serious speaker drowns them out.

"You make fun of him, but you know we have to watch the Russians since they really are spying on us."

Bill's been eager to share his experience in West Virginia and speaks up to get the group's attention.

"My grandfather showed me this place in West Virginia where the government's been eavesdropping on the Russians for more than fifty years. Bill proceeds to relate all he had been told about the "NSA Spy Station."

There's a murmur of excitement in the room and several students speak out.

"Who knows what they're really doing there."

"I'm sure they tap into Chinese and North Korean messages and Iran too."

"What about us real Americans? Are we on the government's radar? Are they spying on us too?"

Judith calls for calm and raises a yellow pad in her right arm. "Sign up now to do the right thing. Let's help make America great again."

She manages to get eight signatures and e-mail addresses and plans to organize a campaign before the 2020 Presidential election.

Once the room empties out, Judith and Bill relax and decide to watch television. Judith plumps up pillows against the wall on the top bunk and Bill clicks the remote hoping to find something romantic.

They're more comfortable with each other now that they hang out alone more often.

Judith's been instructing Bill at the rifle range and he's usually sharing a beer with her afterward. She's been responding to his advances a bit more each Friday night. They've kissed quite often and she's allowed him to fondle her breasts.

"Where's Michael?"

He's still Judith's number one romantic priority.

"He's not coming home tonight. He plans to spend the night with Athena."

An explosion of anger pops in Judith's head as she states dryly. "She never told me they were intimate."

"No they haven't been, but this is it. They've agreed and he's going all out, taking her to a fancy restaurant first. He even bought an engagement ring."

"I have been tricked. Surely God knew what was to transpire with Athena tonight and did not warn me. I

was hoping Judith would succeed and keep him away from Athena, but this is a whole new game."

Zeus leaves and is not privy to Judith's outcry.

"Some best friend. She never said a thing. Well I don't care anymore."

Judith's words hide disappointment at the loss of the love that she thought she had secured last week when she had surprised Michael in his dorm room.

She had planned perfectly. After a few beers she suggested they watch a porn show, claiming she and Bill had done so often.

She was convinced that once they had sex Michael would look at her more favorably and forget Athena.

His words, when he quickly changed the channel, amused her at the time and were even more convincing in her mind of their future together.

"I believe in the sanctity of marriage. We should all save ourselves for that."

She understands his words now.

Angry with Michael and feeling betrayed by her best friend, Judith reaches out to Bill for consolation and the love that she's missing.

THE TEN COMMANDMENTS

Thou shalt have no other gods before me

Thou shalt not make any graven images

Thou shalt not take the Lord's name in vain

Remember the Sabbath day to keep it holy

Honor thy father and thy mother

Thou shalt not kill

Thou shalt not commit adultery

Thou shalt not bear false witness

Thou shalt not steal

Thou shalt not covet thy neighbor's goods

DUELING WITH WORDS

"Zeus, you have been maligning me to my Father. What right do you have to question my purpose and success?"

The priorities in Zeus immortal life have changed drastically overnight.

He has come to the conclusion that the coupling of his Athena and Michael was a plan of God's that he had not been privy to. Nevertheless he wants to take advantage of the opportunity to be included in the new master plan.

He has decided that God intends to use his virgin Athena for a lofty purpose, perhaps even to bear a new Savior and he wishes to lower the position of Jesus.

"You have reached far beyond what God had in mind for you and have allowed all of his commandments to be broken."

"How dare you accuse me? You are a false god. I am the Son of God, true representative of God on earth."

"Ha. That's Commandment Number One right there. You are being worshipped on a higher level. Check out any Christian church and see whose picture is the feature presentation.

"I think that covers Commandment Number Two as well. Your stone statues far outnumber those of God in stone.

"Then there's Number Three…"

"You cannot attribute that to me."

"You may remember that God left you in charge. You are supposed to be the responsible one and you have not prevented the abuse of His name. As for me, I would have sent out quite a few lightning bolts to any who disrespected me.

"I laugh that you couldn't control the next Commandment. Sunday is probably the un-holiest day of the week. Yes, many churches are filled, but what transpires in the earlier hours of Sunday morning?

How many have the odor of alcohol on their breath when taking communion? How much gambling on golf and football games takes place each Sunday afternoon?

"I'll give you the drinking, for I like to sip a cup myself.

"You must admit that your followers failed Number Five. How many parents sit and wait each day for a visit, or just a phone call from a son.

"As far as numbers Six and Seven, not killing or not committing adultery, that's off the chart – no excuses.

"There are many jails filled with people who have stolen, sometimes for stealing food for their hungry family, but take count of those wearing "white collars" who greedily take without punishment or remorse.

"I think that being able to lie with a straight face has become a virtue and giving false testimony is an art.

"Lastly, the Good Will to Thy Neighbor policy. The world is full of bad examples of that.. If it were up to me, I would give you an A for effort and an F for failure."

"The problems on Earth are not of my doing. It is this 'free will' power my Father has bestowed on mankind.

"Mortals have taken the words of wizened men and my disciples written in the time of their ancestors and tried to make them conform to their desires.

"Eye for an eye has become bomb for a bomb. Love for thyself has overcome Love thy Neighbor.

"Honor thy Mother and Father. God's commandments have been buried under a mound of greed.

"Do not think, Zeus, that I am not aware of the state of the universe. I am my Father's son and I feel his foreboding, but my faith has not left me.

"I see millions of good, loving people who are attempting by their deeds to balance the earth. My belief is that each individual's free will has been depressed and abased by money and power but will one day re-surface.

"They cannot express free will while starving or being shot at.

"I do believe I may have misjudged you. But your father's in charge, not me. He's considering throwing in the towel. He's making a last ditch effort to save his creation and you don't look so good."

God had no wish to enter this debate but it was of interest and he has taken in every word.

"YOU DO YOUR BEST TO CONDEMN MY SON. IS THERE SOME THOUGHT IN YOUR HEAD THAT YOU CAN UNSEAT HIM?

"I am so excited. You are so clever and the solution to all the troubles on Earth is at hand.

"WHAT MANNER OF BLUBBERING IS THIS?"

"You are too modest.

"Your Holy Spirit on Earth is pure in heart and mind and the Demi-Goddess Athena, for she surely is, has kept her body pure but for Your Spirit.

"Their coupling last night must be first in your thoughts this morning. Here is our answer.

"In nine months we can begin to save the Earth."

"DO NOT DRAW CONCLUSIONS FOR ME AND DO NOT PRESUME THERE IS ANY 'WE.'

"HAVE YOU CREPT INTO THE MIND OF MY FIRST CHOICE AND BROKEN OUR AGREEMENT?

"The thoughts of the girl Judith were filled throughout the night with the event and I had to conclude that the union of Athena and Michael was in your master plan to have another son.

"Athena is indeed a true demi-goddess and retains her purity. You have kept your new Holy Spirit secret, but I would have gladly approved."

"YOUR ARROGANCE EXCEEDS YOUR IGNORANCE OF MY THOUGHTS."

"I do know your thoughts, Father. Your human is arrogant, prideful, violent, peaceful, vulnerable to evil thoughts, and also filled with good thoughts.

"I'm aware of your young Michael walking the earth and developing his spirituality.

"I'm also aware of his relationship with the young girl, but I do not know if it was your intention to have it end as Zeus suggests.

"If you ask, I would step aside, regrettably but willingly. Making room for another son may be justified if the result balances our world.

"My short life on Earth led me to understand the nature of the human ego. Their sense of importance and self- esteem does not allow man to easily give up on a path they have chosen until fate wields its sword.

"There is very little will to change.

"I also know you were frustrated in the old days when you dealt with sinners by severe measures. If that was all that was needed, I would not have come to be.

"No, father, my sacrifice was not in vain.

"But have you forgotten forgiveness of sins, the very heart of my sacrifice?

"I know You are disappointed with the world and it sometimes overtakes me as well.

"It helps me to make sure my presence known at every birth. I rejoice at the moment that each new earthling appears. There's another tiny bit of hope each time.

"I am secure in the thought that one of them, of any race or religion, can become a savior to their people, with or without our assistance.

"The world is in an age of violence and upheaval. Your young man has pointed out the

record number of natural disasters in his short lifetime. It may be that man is mimicking nature, or nature is being assisted in its devastation by man.

"I did wonder why man gave the natural events human names, but it is fitting. Man is truly one with the Earth and its nature, along with some flaws.

"You have chosen well.

"The thoughts and deeds of these twelve young people are a microcosm of the happenings in the universe.

"You are right to place the fate of the world in the hands of the young."

Zeus no longer feels the need to belittle the work of Jesus. He retreats to consider his new approach.

PRO'S AND CON'S

"IT'S BEEN ALMOST TWO YEARS AND IT SEEMS THAT OUR TWELVE DO STILL FOLLOW A PATTERN OF IMBALANCE THAT HAS BEEN LAID DOWN FOR CENTURIES BY MAN. THEY DO GOOD, THEY DO EVIL. NO DO NOTHING TO EFFECT REAL CHANGE."

"A year or two means very little in the ocean of time. They will succeed, have patience."

Zeus has no wish to lose the foothold back into the world he foresees through his "daughter" Athena's unborn child. His mind is racing but he hides his thoughts.

"The prize is beyond my dreams.

"Immortality would no longer be a bore, but would now lead to everlasting pleasure as I watch each new generation of demi-gods emerge.

"My power would return if only in my palace above the clouds. Immortality would become sweet once more. I must handle this with care."

"MY FEARS HAVE NOT ABATED AND MY COURSE IS NOT CLEAR. I AM DIVIDED IN MY THOUGHTS JUST AS THE PEOPLE OF THE WORLD ARE DIVIDED IN THOUGHT AND DEED. MY WORDS HAVE BEEN MISUSED AND DISOBEYED AND IN THE PROCESS HAVE RESULTED IN A MEANING IN WHICH LOVE, FORGIVENESS, AND RESPECT HAVE BEEN PUT ASIDE."

Zeus knows that he must keep calm now and be convincing.

"You have seen the world rise to embrace your first son. Many generations have prospered under his guidance."

"YOU CHANGE YOUR TUNE, BUT WHAT YOU SAY IS TRUE.

"WHAT OF MANKIND'S PROBLEM OF NOT BEING ABLE TO BALANCE THE NATURE OF EARTH WITH ITS OWN GREEDY APPETITE?

"THE WATERS HAVE BEEN FOULED. THE ABUNDANCE OF FISH THAT THE TWELVE DISCIPLES DIPPED THEIR NETS INTO HAVE DWINDLED AND CLEAN WATER TO DRINK IS ALREADY SCARCE.

"POLLUTION IN THE AIR IS BEING MONITORED CLOSELY AS THOUGH A POINT BELOW THAT OF THE DAY BEFORE MEANS SUFFICIENT PROGRESS AND SOLUTIONS ARE PUT OFF FOR FUTURE GENERATIONS TO DEAL WITH.

"THEY ABSORB THE SHUDDERING OF THE EARTH THEY WALK ON WITHOUT FULLY UNDERSTANDING THE EFFECTS.

"IF THE VOLCANIC ERUPTIONS DO NOT BRING THE END ABOUT, THEY MAY WELL DO IT THEMSELVES WITH THEIR FORMIDABLE ARSENALS."

Zeus is despondent. He knows that he must quash these negative thoughts and show that the best course is the new savior. He tries a more gentle approach.

"You made a wise decision in choosing a mortal woman to mother Jesus. Now the young Athena has the attributes required to be the holy vessel. Your new child will be a leader and his earthly father will guide him as your holy spirit.

"Your First Son has already agreed that he would step aside. He need not disappear.

" He could guide as a big brother. A new son will bring renewed vitality and would lead to the balance you desire.

"This time no sacrifice is needed. The new Christ will be born to the 'Angel of the People' and my Athena, his pure wife.

"You were drawn to Michael and gave him insight to you. You will have time to groom the child."

"He will be ready just as the predicted time the earth would self-destruct is on the horizon. He will be accepted world wide as the Savior every religion awaits. With your blessing all the congregations of the churches, synagogues, mosques, shrines and temples will rejoice.

"It has worked many times before. You said so. Remember me, Ba'al, and all the others who have come and gone. It is the natural course of events.

"Michael is very bright and has gained strength with his new found celebrity. Certainly his idea of making use of the natural resources of the asteroids would be of great assistance in renewing Earth's depleted resources."

"I'M NOT SURE THAT HIS THOUGHTS TO EXTEND THE HABITAT OF EARTH INTO THE UNIVERSE ARE THE BEST COURSE.

"WOULD HE CONTINUE TO REPRESENT MY WILL, OR WOULD HIS FREE WILL BE MAKING ALL THE DECISIONS?

"HIS OWN FREELY WILLED DESIRE COULD BECOME A NEED FOR THE PERSONAL

FAME AND FORTUNE INVOLVED IN HIS MOVING THE PEOPLE OF EARTH TO MARS.

"DO I THEN DESTROY THE EARTH AND THOSE WHO CHOOSE NOT TO FOLLOW HIM?

"OR DO ALLOW EARTH TO REMAIN ON ITS PATH TO SELF DESTRUCTION?

"WHAT ABOUT THE THOUGHTS OF THE YOUNG ATHENA? I HAVE NOT TOUCHED ON THEM."

"We have seen that all her thoughts and actions are pure. Surely she is perfect to be the right hand of Michael and the perfect mother to your son."

"WOULD ALL DECISIONS BE OUT OF MY HANDS?"

Zeus sarcasm rises to the fore. He is growing impatient.

"Have the decisions on earth not been out of your hands for many generations?

"By your own admission, you may have lost control."

"WHAT OF MY COMMITMENT TO THE TWELVE WE CHOSE?

"DO I ERASE THEIR GOOD AND BAD DEEDS IN THE DECISION MAKING PROCESS? THEY REPRESENT THE WORLD. DO I ERASE THEM ALONG WITH IT?"

"They may well continue with their roles by fulfilling them as disciples."

"DISCIPLES, IS IT!

"OR DID YOU HAVE THE TITLE GOD AND GODDESSES IN MIND."

Zeus quickly changes the subject to avoid any more of his thoughts being uncovered.

"The Sun was from the beginning of time part of the world's existence. The appearance of New Suns in the ancient world and in the Sun Stone of the Aztecs meant an end to chaos and renewed vitality.

"It is a play on words, but a new Son would mean as much today.

"WHAT SAY YOU, FIRST SON?

"SHALL IT MEAN YOU SHARING THE TEACHING, HOPING FOR WORLD WIDE REPENTANCE?

"WOULD THE WORLD BE FICKLE AND REJECT YOU IN FAVOR OF A YOUNGER VERSION AS THEY MIGHT A MOVIE STAR?"

"Father, you have been served well for many thousands of years in many different cultures under many different names. However, 'Them and Us' has became the byword, not only of religious beliefs, but in the equality of man, the liberty of women, the very right to sustenance.

"My cross divides major religions. The wars before the time of my sacrifice were for power and property. My suffering and the Crusades made a huge imprint and changed the reasons man gives for waging war.

"The cross was never meant to divide people. It was never intended to cause wars.

"The New Testament of the Bible covers my lifetime on Earth. It is filled with stories of the meaning of life, of my healing, of my preaching and teaching my disciples to carry my messages on. Many of those messages have been buried.

"Your message was one of forgiveness of sins. I was the lamb of sacrifice. Some might say, why love a sinner, or more to the point, why did I love sinners enough to sacrifice my life for them.

"My mortality at that time gave me the essence of free will. I was tempted and could have relied on their mercy and supplicated myself to the will of the powerful.

"The word crucial is derived from crux, meaning cross.

"The crux of the matter is that now it is crucial to bridge the divide.

"What's done cannot be undone. Religious factions must learn to love unconditionally.

"Would you cry out to a fireman who tries to pick you up and carry you out of a burning building, "Wait, what are your religious beliefs?

"There are many Jesuses making sacrifices in the world today. The soldier running into battle, the

policeman confronting armed criminals, the fireman entering a home or a forest on fire, a doctor volunteering in a disease ridden village, a nurse binding bleeding wounds, a mother protecting her child.

"Jesus comes with many names, in different shapes, sizes and colors. Every Jesus loves without question and there is an abundance of them on Earth.

"However, I do see that change is inevitable and I would welcome a new Savior with open arms.

"Father, the decision is yours to make."

FREE WILL

Athena is behind the wheel at the moment. She and Judith have been taking turns driving for several hours. They're debating each other while considering their own choices, sometimes arguing and sometimes silent, never quite agreeing.

Last month they had bumped into each other at the pharmacy counter, both asking about the "day after pill." Hearing the disheartening news that the pill's effectiveness lasts no longer than five days, they went back to the dorm with testing packages in their backpacks. Both their pregnancies, acquired at about the same time, are just past the ten week mark.

Judith had been avoiding Athena for weeks since she and Bill had been together.

It was only when Athena told her that she had not accepted Michael's marriage proposal because she felt they were too young that Judith softened and embraced Athena, her best friend once more.

Athena confided to Judith that she and Michael actually only "did it" once, so she didn't believe she was pregnant.

"There must be some other reason I skipped my period."

"Who are you kidding? We're both like clockwork. We haven't missed in years, even shared the same days after we moved in together.

"I should worry more. Bill and I did it more often, but the first time we didn't have a condom handy and took a chance. I sure don't want to have a baby yet or get married now."

"Your car has two "Pro-Life" bumper stickers and you're a poster child for the Conservatives wanting to get rid of Roe v. Wade. What are you thinking?"

Here they were now, each holding a stick of the wrong color considering what they should do. They had stopped and tested once more even though they were quite sure by now. Pamphlets meant to be helpful are strewn all over the floor of the jeep.

"I do believe in a woman's free choice. I haven't even told Michael.

"Actually I haven't seen much of him since we were together. I'm not sure who's avoiding who."

"It's early. My stomach is still flat. I don't look pregnant.

"There are two girls on our dorm floor that swear they've had abortions. They look okay. If they didn't tell, no one would know.

"As for Bill, I have to make up my own mind before I decide to tell him or not."

"My parents would kill me. But they'd kill me if I stay pregnant too. I'm dead either way. I've barely started living myself, what would I do with a baby."

"No, No Athena is the chosen one to bear the child that will save the world. It's her sacred duty.

"Just think my grandson could be the next Son of God. What a glorious thought.

"YOUR THINKING IS INCONSISTENT WITH THE FACTS. ALTHOUGH HER BLOOD MAY BE SHARED WITH THE ANCIENT GREEKS, THERE IS NO REASON TO BELIEVE THAT ATHENA IS YOUR DESCENDANT.

"MICHAEL AND ATHENA HAVE MATED, HOWEVER WE OFTEN SEE THAT THE WORLD DOES NOT ACCEPT OR VALUE THE CHILD OF AN UNWED MOTHER, NOR THE MOTHER HERSELF.

"BUT THERE WILL ALWAYS BE ROOM ON EARTH FOR ANOTHER CHILD, PERHAPS ANOTHER SAVIOR."

"Oh Judith, I do wish my mother were here if only to hug me and tell me everything will be alright even though I know it's not."

"I haven't thought about my mother for a while. It took a lot of therapy to be able to go through Grandma's photo albums and feel a connection to the woman in the pictures holding an infant – me.

"It seems that for years I blamed them for leaving me, as though my Dad should have avoided the accident. I had a dream about them last night.

They were smiling at each other and Dad was pushing me on a swing. I cried and had a tantrum when my mother said it was time to go. I insisted on swinging some more."

"I'm sorry your mother died when you were so young. I don't know what I would have done growing up without mine.

"She always had answers to the little things that went wrong but this is my big problem, no one else's."

"Well, we can't wait any longer. We've been over every angle and scenario. So it's time."

The jeep was backed easily into a parking spot facing a pink brick building with very large blue letters over the glass door entryway.

"PLANNED PARENTHOOD"

Disappointed and upset at the turn of events, Zeus projects his anger elsewhere.

"There goes your solution. Your first son is a sham, not worthy of the position, and now we may be losing our chance."

"*OUR* CHANCE?"

"Why have you brought us to this point? What was your purpose?

"We watched the future of the world in the actions of the twelve young mortals we chose. When we tested them admittedly not all of them did so well, but we were impressed with the actions of most.

"Now it's time for Athena to come through for us and for you to allow the world to continue."

It's a windy day and both girls are wearing their school jackets.

It's hard to say if it's a red head or brunette leaving the car and heading for the glass doors since the hood of her jacket is pulled tight around her head.

"I'm not going in, but I'll come back for you later."

The lime green jeep Wrangler speeds out of the parking lot, as though trying to leave unresolved thoughts behind in its wake.

"You do not seem upset. Is that because you made the decision and know the outcome already?

"Will you sit back and await your new son?

"Upon reflection, I see now why you chose me to help you. You saw man in me, not a god. I had strength and weakness, avarice, desire, and much power.

"I had the power to destroy, the power to kill, the power to provoke anger in others and to bring it forth in myself.

"I had the power to deny, the power to give generously, the power for good, the power for evil.

"I was blessed and also cursed with the emotions that enrich and plague man. Most of all, I had the power of free will.

"All the powers that I had exist in man and always did. I may be a mythical figure, but mankind is well depicted in those myths."

"Yes, that was it. You chose me because you saw the example of man in me!

"WHY DID I CHOOSE YOU? INDEED YOU WERE AN EXAMPLE OF MAN AS YOU SAY, BUT YOUR REIGN'S BALANCE WAS OF MORE INTEREST TO ME.

"HOMER MAY HAVE FASHIONED HIS TALES AFTER REALITY AND HE SEEMS TO HAVE COVERED THE HISTORY OF BLESSINGS AND FAULTS OF MORTALS IN DESCRIBING YOUR GODS.

"THE DEMOCRATIC IDEALS OF EQUAL STATUS OF CITIZENS, INCLUDING WOMEN, AND PUBLIC EDUCATION IN YOUR TIME LED TO ADVANCES IN PHILOSOPHY, MEDICINE, ART, ASTRONOMY AND MUCH MORE.

"HOWEVER EVIL DID FIND ITS WAY INTO THE BALANCE AND THE SCALES OF GOOD AND EVIL WERE IN PLAY.

"YOU ARE RIGHT.

"YOU MAY HAVE REMAINED ON YOUR THRONE FOR A MUCH LONGER TIME, BUT ONLY IF EVIL HAD NOT PREVAILED ON THE PART OF THE LEADERS OF YOUR WORLD.

"WHEN WE BEGAN OUR QUEST, THE EARTH WAS OUT OF BALANCE. IT WAS EVIDENT THAT IT HAD COME TO THE POINT THAT IT WOULD EVENTUALLY DESTROY ITSELF BY ITS OWN ACTIONS.

"OUR CHOSEN DOZEN MORTALS HAVE ILLUSTRATED MANY OF THE PROBLEMS THAT BESET EARTH. THEY HAVE ENDURED THE EVILS FLUNG AT THEM AND THEY HAVE MADE CHOICES, BOTH GOOD AND BAD.

"THEY REMAIN, NOT UNSCATHED, BUT MORE IDEALISTIC THAN PREVIOUS GENERATIONS IN THEIR PHILOSOPHY OF MANKIND'S RESPONSIBILITY TO CARE FOR EACH OTHER AND THE WORLD THEY LIVE IN.

"ZEUS, IT DOES NOT MATTER WHO IS DRIVING AWAY AND WHO CHOSE TO GO INSIDE.

"THE UNIVERSE IS WHOLE AND MAN AND EARTH ARE INTEGRAL PARTS OF IT.

"IF THERE IS TO BE A SAVIOR, IT WILL BE BY CHOICE, BY THE FREE WILL OF THE PEOPLE OF EARTH."

"I do believe you knew all along that it was worth saving and was seeking the reassurance that we found in the young people we chose."

"DECISIONS WILL CONTINUE TO BE MADE AND THE WORLD WILL CONTINUE TO EXIST BUT ONLY IF IT REACHES THE POINT THAT THE SCALES REQUIRE.

"IT IS THE BALANCE OF THE WORLD THAT REMAINS TO BE ACHIEVED."

"I can see you no longer have need of me. I will have much time to reflect on our journey and shall look for the hope loosed from Pandora's box.

The giant eagle that leaves the scene, turning once to make a final sweep, believes he hears a soft voice as he heads toward Mt. Olympus.

"GOD SPEED"

Ω